"If you're not ha
Pandora took i
drying a sauce

"Did I say that?" *I can't even say why, but my gut tells me you're hiding something.*

"You've seen my references. If I've caused you to doubt my ability to care for your son, then—"

"Dammit, Pandora." When he slapped his palm to the table, she not only jumped, but tears filled her eyes. He was instantly sorry, yet at the same time, he'd been trained to always follow his instincts. What was going on with her that he couldn't see? "What's with you? Some things don't add up. Your first day on the job, when you didn't have a cell or a way to even purchase a small amount of groceries without calling me for help. The fact that you lived in Norfolk, yet have never been to the beach. Your two mystery Saturdays. All I'm asking is for you to be straight with me. Is there something going on with you that I'm missing?"

"No." She raised her chin, and her expression lost its earlier wide-eyed fear and turned to steely determination. "But if you're unhappy with my performance, I'll turn in my resignation in the morning."

Dear Reader,

This story features a character and issue *much* heavier than I've ever dared deal with before. The character is Pandora from the first book in my Operation: Family series, *A SEAL's Secret Baby.* Her issue is serious alcoholism. By the end of that first book, her volunteer counselor, Ellie, feared Pandora was a lost cause.

What Ellie failed to take into account was the strength of a mother's love. It's no secret I'm a big ol' momma bear when it comes to my kids, and Pandora discovers she's no different. Alas, she also finds that just because she knows she's no longer the addict who once lost her child, that doesn't mean the rest of the world will be so accepting.

What I never expected was how personal this story became. When we took in our son, Russell, we found ourselves on the opposite end of just such a heartbreaking situation in that we were the court-appointed family who received a dear child.

I can't fathom how tough being a social worker must be. One time through this process was more than enough for me. My hearts goes out to all the men and women striving to reunite families who've lost their way.

As for Pandora and Calder, you'll have to read on to discover if their sweet, unexpected family finds their happy ending....

Happy reading!

Laura Marie

A NAVY SEAL'S
SURPRISE BABY

—

LAURA MARIE ALTOM

HARLEQUIN® AMERICAN ROMANCE®

Recycling programs
for this product may
not exist in your area.

ISBN-13: 978-0-373-75470-0

A NAVY SEAL'S SURPRISE BABY

Copyright © 2013 by Laura Marie Altom

Printed in U.S.A.

ABOUT THE AUTHOR

After college (Go, Hogs!), bestselling, award-winning author Laura Marie Altom did a brief stint as an interior designer before becoming a stay-at-home mom to boy-girl twins and a bonus son. Always an avid romance reader, she knew it was time to try her hand at writing when she found herself replotting the afternoon soaps.

When not immersed in her next story, Laura teaches art at a local middle school. In her free time she beats her kids at video games, tackles Mount Laundry and, of course, reads romance!

Laura loves hearing from readers at either P.O. Box 2074, Tulsa, OK 74101, or by email, BaliPalm@aol.com.

Love winning fun stuff? Check out www.lauramariealtom.com.

Books by Laura Marie Altom

*U.S. Marshals
**Baby Boom
***The Buckhorn Ranch
‡Operation: Family

This story is dedicated to all of my
new Twitter friends on #YR.

From the day *The Young & The Restless* began,
I've watched with my mother. My daughter has now
joined in and even though they'd never admit it, the
guys in our family occasionally follow along, too! The
characters of this long-running daytime show have
become like family to me, and 11:00 a.m. to 12:00
noon each day has become sacred! LOL!

Since discovering Twitter, I've found a great wealth
of fellow *Y & R* viewers who are always eager to
discuss Genoa City's latest gossip. As an added
bonus, many have also become great friends.

Here's to you *Y & R!* May your rich, wonderful
characters be forever young and *especially* restless!

Chapter One

Pandora?

One glance at the next name on his nanny-candidate list told navy SEAL Calder Remington all he needed to know. She'd be a card-carrying unicorn lover or flake. He needed a Mary or Hazel. Someone not only dependable, but with impeccable references and the patience of Mother Teresa. The last four women had been nice enough, but they'd lacked experience. Ideally, he needed a grandmotherly type who'd successfully raised her own brood to be doctors, and now looked to pass along her vast parental knowledge to the next generation.

At twenty-eight, how much parenting knowledge could Pandora have?

Calder had pretty much resigned himself to not even let her in the house when the doorbell rang. He dropped his list and sighed. In light of the fluid situation, he adjusted his mission to ditching *Pandora* quickly enough to allow time for a nap before the next candidate showed.

Calder glanced at eight-month-old Quinn, who played on the floor with his favorite stuffed whale. "Might as well get this over with, huh, buddy?"

"Gah!"

Calder shook his head. "My thoughts exactly."

He opened the door on a petite brunette whose black-rimmed glasses struck him as too big for her face. "Um, hello. I, ah, was sent by the Earth Angels agency to—"

"Appreciate your stopping by—" the August heat coming in the door already made him break out in a sweat "—but I need someone older."

"Oh…." As if she were a leaky balloon, her shoulders deflated. "Maybe if you would just give me a chance? You know, like try my services for a week, then decide?"

Desperation fairly oozed from her pores. "Kind of you to offer, but—"

He didn't think it possible, but when she glanced past him into the house, her complexion paled. He was shocked when she shoved him out of her way to sprint across the living room as if she'd just caught a Hail Mary pass and was intent on snagging a game-winning touchdown.

He turned to see what kind of nut-job stunt she was pulling, only to go weak at the knees. Quinn had turned blue. Pandora scooped him into her arms and turned him upside down. She delivered five raps on his back, then flipped him over to do the same in the front. No results.

Calder might be a navy SEAL and combat veteran, but he had never felt more helpless. Since May, he'd been meaning to take an infant first-aid class, but between work and single-dad duties, it was almost September and he still hadn't found time.

She repositioned his son once more and then like magic, a grape popped from Quinn's mouth onto the carpeted floor.

While Calder gaped, Quinn wailed.

Pandora hugged Calder's panicked son, rocking him gently, calming him with a soft, sweet lullaby in his ear.

Once his son's cries had been reduced to occasional shuddering huffs, she held out her hand for Calder to shake. "I'm sorry. In all the excitement, I failed to properly introduce myself. I'm Pandora Moore."

Still shaky, Calder shook the woman's hand. This certainly put a new spin on the situation. How did his conscience justify sending her on her way when she'd literally saved Quinn's life? Did he repay that debt by flat out giving her the job? "Nice to meet you. Calder Remington." Pointing to his son, he asked, "Where'd you learn that—the baby Heimlich thing?"

"Basic Infant Care 101. Choking is a leading cause of infant mortality—which is beyond tragic considering most cases are preventable." She took the bowl of grapes from the coffee table, placing them on the mantel.

"Yeah, well, you made me feel pretty stupid." He rammed his hands into his jeans pockets.

"Oh, no, I didn't mean to imply you're a bad parent."

"I get it." Whether she'd meant it or not, her words stung because Calder knew them to be true. He may be good at a lot of things, but raising a kid wasn't one. He tried, but even after having had Quinn for a few months, nothing about it felt natural. Bottom line, Calder had wearied of the whole nanny search. Unable to shake the guilt telling him the least he could do for this woman who'd saved his son was give her a chance, he asked, "How soon can you start?"

Her eyebrows rose. "You mean you want me for the job?"

"Sure. We'll give it a try." He still didn't wholly trust a woman named *Pandora,* but guys on his team were always giving him crap for his name. Didn't seem fair for him to turn around and do the same. "Can you start first thing tomorrow?"

She pushed up her glasses and shyly smiled. "Sure. The agency said it's a live-in position, right?"

"Yeah." He gestured down the hall. "Follow me. I'll show you your room."

STANDING IN THE sunshine-flooded bedroom with its own private bath and even a bay window peering out on the grassy, tree-lined backyard, Pandora fought the urge to pinch herself. A hardwood dresser, nightstand and headboard all matched and the tan carpet was clean enough for the baby in her arms to crawl wherever he wanted—assuming there weren't more grapes lying around. The queen-size mattress was bare, but new enough to still wear furniture-store stickers.

After all she'd been through, this felt surreal. As a bonus, Calder even seemed like a great guy. Though he possessed beyond steal-your-breath good looks, her gut told her he was a gentleman. As for the indefinable jolt of awareness stemming from just shaking his hand? She was determined to push that from her mind.

"Don't blame you if you hate the color," he said in regard to the mixed shades of lavender, orange and lime green polluting the walls. "The last owner went a little crazy with their sponge painting. We'll pick out something more to your liking."

"Yellow," she automatically said. "I've always wanted a room the shade of lemon sorbet."

He laughed. "You got it. As for the bedspread, towels, sheets and everything, I figured you'd be more comfortable using your own."

"Yes. Thanks." Only trouble was, she didn't have her own. But she had managed to save some money. It wouldn't hurt to spend a smidge of her precious savings on the perfect floral comforter set to match her soon-to-be newly painted walls.

Quinn had fallen asleep in her arms.

The sensation of once again holding an infant struck her as sublime.

For the past year, she'd held a steady after-school childcare position until the Norfolk naval family had been transferred overseas. Pandora's charges had been two little girls aged five and seven. During that time and up to the present, she lived at a halfway house in a gloomy basement bedroom no bigger than some closets. The enormity of this job and all the secondary perks it entailed were too great to presently absorb, so she held them close as she might have a secret gift she wouldn't open until she had some privacy. No, she wouldn't even think about the full ramifications until Calder signed the agency paperwork that officially brought her dream one step closer to fruition.

"Want me to take him?" Her new boss nodded to his son before leading Pandora into the hall.

"Thanks, but I'm good." And she was. Nuzzling the infant's downy hair, she drank in his familiar baby smells of lotion and powder. If this angel were truly hers, she'd never let him go. "If it's not too personal, where's Quinn's mom?"

Calder's expression darkened as he said, "Not to be evasive, but that's a long story best told over a few beers."

"Oh." He drank? She'd hoped he didn't, but that was probably expecting too much.

"Come on. I'll show you Quinn's room and the rest of the house. We've only been here a few weeks. My schedule made it tough to nail down the closing date."

"You work a lot of overtime?"

He snorted as he led the way into a surprisingly drab nursery. "Guess you could call it that. Sorry—I'm still off my game from the whole choking thing. I'm a navy SEAL. A big part of my job is being called out with little or no notice. Like, I might tell you I'll be home for dinner, but then get assigned a mission and won't be back for six months— granted, it's usually not that long, but it can happen. Technically, for just that reason, my mom has shared custody of Quinn. But since she's in North Carolina, I need you here for any and all immediate contingencies. That's why it was important for me to hire someone through an agency. I need to know you're not only reliable and great with my kid, but have the kind of stable history and experience in caring for children that allows me to be one hundred percent certain you're doing a great job. That way, I can fully focus on what I do, which makes my life a helluva lot saner."

Pandora wished she were as confident with the trust he placed in her as Calder. Though in her head, she'd put her past firmly behind her, in her heart the fallout still remained.

Rocking Quinn, she asked, "How can you stand being away from this cutie?"

For a split second, Calder looked blank. "I, ah, guess for what I do, I don't have a lot of options. Come on, I'll show you the kitchen."

Pandora followed, trailing her fingertips along white walls. Had Calder already painted the hall? Somehow she couldn't imagine the same person who'd attacked her room with color being satisfied with a vanilla thoroughfare.

In the kitchen, Calder said, "Nothing fancy here. I don't expect you to cook for me. Just make sure Quinn gets decent meals. I set up a household account at the bank. You can use it for groceries, diapers—whatever else we need around here or for Quinn."

She nodded, though inside, she felt as if she may be dreaming. How many nights had she gone to bed hungry because she had no cash for food?

You sure managed to scrape up enough dough for other things, her conscience was all too happy to point out.

Fighting fire with fire, she squelched the seemingly constant voice in her head, reminding her she was destined to fail, by saying, "Thanks again for this opportunity. I'll care for Quinn as if he were my own."

Wrong choice of words considering what had happened to her sweet Julia. She squelched that thought, too.

"I'm pretty sure I should be thanking you." He fished a key from a meticulously organized drawer, handing it to her. "Everyone I know with kids says the agency you work for doesn't fool around when it comes to hiring the most qualified people."

Pandora knew that to be true. Her best friend, Natalie, put all of her employees through extensive background checks. She feared the only reason Natalie had hired Pandora was because of the friendship they'd struck up at the restaurant where Pandora waited tables. But no matter how many times Natalie assured Pandora that wasn't the case, or how much additional training she'd done on her own, she never quite felt part of acceptable society—or worthy of receiving good fortune.

"WELL? YOU EVER going to tell me how the interview went?"

Pandora glanced up from cramming her few books into a box to find Natalie seated on the halfway house's twin bed. She may have offered to help, but so far had done nothing but talk. "Obviously, it was good, or Calder wouldn't have hired me."

"Duh. I'm the one who filled out the paperwork. I want the inside scoop. Did you find out what happened with Quinn's mom? I kept waiting for an explanation, but he never told me."

"I asked, but Calder said he'd talk about it later." Pandora purposely left out the part about the beers. No need for her friend to worry about her returning to the dark side.

"Interesting." Natalie tapped her index finger against her lips. "Wonder what happened for her to leave? The guy's so handsome it hurts to look at him. Don't you think?"

"No," Pandora lied. In truth, not only was Calder easy on the eyes, but her cheeks flamed at the mere memory of the heat caused by just shaking his hand. "Even if I did, what would I do about it? Don't you have a strict nonfraternization policy with clients?"

"True, and I appreciate you pointing that out, but you'd

have to be a zombie not to have at least noticed that killer grin—and the width of his shoulders. Dear Lord…" Natalie fanned herself.

Pandora pitched a pillow at her usually more serious friend. "Knock it off. All you need to know is that Calder seems to be a great guy, and the fact that he hired me is a miracle." She swallowed hard to keep the tears at bay.

"You deserve every ounce of good that's been happening for you lately." Standing, her friend ambushed Pandora with a sideways hug. "I never would've suggested you for this job if I didn't think you were capable of handling it."

"Thanks." Pandora sniffled and nodded. "But it's hard, you know? And I didn't expect that. For years, I've dreamed of living a normal life and now that I'm getting out of here and moving into this adorable home with an even cuter baby, I…" Her blessings plate felt inordinately full. The only thing missing was her daughter. But not for long, she promised herself.

PANDORA WOKE THE next morning at five. Calder said she didn't need to be at his house until seven, but excitement refused to grant another minute's sleep.

She and Natalie had packed all her belongings into five boxes—including her toiletries. Calder had offered to help her move, but she was embarrassed not only about where she lived, but how little she actually owned, so she'd declined.

She took a quick shower, dressed, brushed her teeth, blow-dried her hair and put it in a quick ponytail and carted the boxes to her car, then stripped her bed, swept the floor and wiped down all flat surfaces. Since she'd spoken with the house counselor and completed all necessary release paperwork the previous night, by six, she'd said her goodbyes to the few women who were awake, then turned in her key. Once in her car, headed toward her new home, she never looked back.

That part of her life was over and she never wanted to revisit it. Never wanted the shame of being forced by her own poor choices to live in a group home again.

She merged onto the highway and made it to Calder's Norfolk neighborhood thirty-five minutes ahead of schedule. She passed the time by driving around, admiring the tidy neighborhood and park close enough for her to take Quinn to play. She'd have so much fun caring for him and Calder's home that it hardly seemed fair for her to accept a salary.

Pulling her car into Calder's driveway filled her with a kind of quiet satisfaction she'd never known. The only thing better would be having a home of her own—which she would, but this made a great first step.

The redbrick house featured large-paned windows with white shutters. The postage-stamp-size yard was neat with box hedges lining the foundation, but the flower beds were bare save for a few hardy weeds. She wondered if Calder would mind if she and Quinn planted fall flowers. She'd always loved pansies.

"Hey, you're early."

Pandora had been deep in her daydream when her new boss stepped barefoot and bare chested onto the front porch. Wearing khaki cargo pants, he carried a sleepy Quinn still dressed in footy pajamas. If she'd thought the home a lovely sight, the man and his son were downright mesmerizing. Mouth dry, she took a moment to even form words. It sounded cliché, but she honestly hadn't known men had arms and chests so muscular outside of movies.

Quinn rubbed his eyes and whimpered.

"He's been cranky this morning." Calder took the few porch steps with ease, offering her his son. "You handle him and I'll unload your stuff."

"I—I can get it." Would he find it odd she owned so few belongings? "I don't want you to go to any trouble."

"No worries." Handing her the baby, he said, "We're in this together now." Eyeing the barely full backseat, he asked, "This it? Or do you have a friend with a truck coming later?"

"That's all." She jiggled Quinn, coaxing out a smile.

The infant grabbed her glasses, giggling while trying to shove them in his mouth.

"Whoa," she said with a laugh. "If you want breakfast, I'm going to need those."

Calder strolled past her with a box of books so heavy she'd had to take rest stops every few feet. He eyed her funnily. Longer than usual. Was everything okay? He couldn't tell from just the acrid smell lingering on her belongings where she'd been living, could he? A lot of the women had smoked heavily. Sometimes, Pandora feared she might never rid herself of the stench.

On his way into the house, Calder said, "I left a credit card for you on the kitchen table. Quinn's seriously low on baby food and formula and stuff, so you'll probably need to fix that situation and grab anything you want for yourself. I usually get fast food on the way home. If you run into trouble, just call my cell. Number's on the fridge. What's your number?"

"I, ah, don't have one." Too expensive. She'd made her Saturday calls to Julia on the pay phone outside the half-way house.

"Wow, okay. Well, we'll work on that. Also, while the weather's nice, use my SUV since it has Quinn's car seat and stroller. Keys are hanging on a rack by the garage door. Oh—and you might as well park your car in the garage. There should be plenty of room."

Toying with the bear on the tummy of Quinn's pj's, she asked, "How will you get to work?"

"Motorcycle. Usually only use it on the weekends, but this'll give me a great excuse to ride."

"Oh." His shoulders, chest and arms were so tanned. Did

he do a lot of work outdoors? Was it wrong she had a tough time focusing on anything but his sheer, male magnificence?

"SHE HOT?" Calder's friend and fellow SEAL team member, Mason Brown—also known as "Snowman" because he grew up in Alaska and never got cold— finished his bologna sandwich and tossed the wrapper from three-point range into the trash. He missed.

"Who?" Calder asked as he opened a bag of chips. They'd been stuck in a classroom studying smart-bomb mechanisms all morning. The fresh air felt good. Plus, the day was pretty nice for a change—not too hot. They shared a picnic table with their other friends.

Across from Calder sat Heath "Hopper" Stone, nickname earned from his knack for hopping over any obstacle while at a full-on run.

Next to him, Cooper "Cowboy" Hansen. Rumor had him riding into Basic Underwater Demolition—affectionately known as BUDs—on horseback, but Calder always figured he'd just grown up on a ranch.

The group was rounded out by a bunch of boring-ass married guys who talked about nothing but their wives and kids. Deacon and Garrett used to be fun, but lately Calder had to force himself to even be normal around them. Oh, he loved Quinn because he was his son, but he also loved the life he'd made for himself.

Commitment wasn't his thing.

He sure as hell didn't want to hear about the so-called promised land of marriage. What a joke. Besides, for all practical purposes he was married—to the navy.

He loved his job. He loved how being a SEAL made the ladies go weak in the knees—not that he bragged about being a SEAL. That wouldn't be cool. But they were a different breed and women smelled them from a mile away. Adrenaline rushes and seeing the world were his life. Before Quinn, the apartment he'd shared with Mason, Heath and Cooper had only been a temporary layover between adventures.

"Duh," Heath said, "the nanny. Is she hot?"

Mason groaned. "Nannies rank right up there with kindergarten teachers on the sexy meter. I like to think there's a whole lot of naughtiness going on under all that nice."

Calder crossed his arms and glared. "Show some respect here, people. She's nice—and really knows her stuff around Quinn." And though he sure as hell wouldn't mention it to this crew, when Quinn had helped himself to Pandora's glasses, and she'd laughed, Calder had been forced to do a double take. In that moment, with the morning sun making her complexion glow, holding his giggling son, she'd been genuinely pretty. Wholesome. Exactly the look he wanted for his son. "I'm lucky to have found her and wouldn't even think of screwing up a good working relationship by making it personal."

Mason roared. "Just keep tellin' yourself that, man."

"Keep it down," Garrett snapped from the other end of the table. He and his wife, Eve, had just had a baby boy and Garrett was obsessed with showing everyone his latest cellphone videos. "My son's talking…"

Calder shook his head. As the parent of his own infant, he knew kids were far from expert communicators. Guilt consumed him for not feeling more in regard to his son. What was wrong with him? When Pandora asked how Calder stood being away from Quinn, he hadn't had a good answer. Single-handedly caring for an infant was so stressful, whenever he got the chance to bolt, he did.

So why didn't he miss his baby and take hundreds of pictures of Quinn? Most days, Calder felt as if he lacked the most basic of dad genes. Probably had something to do with the way Quinn had abruptly entered his world.

But now that he'd finally found a nanny, he could do right by his son while at the same time getting back to what he did best. Killing terrorists with his guns, then slaying the ladies with his looks.

Chapter Two

When Calder left that morning, for Pandora the house took on the almost-reverent peace she'd only previously found in a church. Maybe it was because of the sun streaming through the many-paned windows? Or could it be as mundane a reason as her boss had painted most of the house angelic white? Regardless, she held Quinn on her hip, kicking off her sandals carefully, quietly taking it all in.

She admired the honeyed glow of maple floors in the kitchen, den and entry. In the living room, the carpet caressed her bare feet like crushed velvet. The brown leather couch and armchair still had tags hanging from them. The coffee table and a flat-panel TV sitting atop a wood stand were the room's only other pieces. Calder mentioned he and Quinn hadn't lived in the house long. Was he taking his time finding more stuff? Waiting till he had money in his budget? Or did he genuinely not care whether or not his house felt like a home?

She hoped he didn't want to rush a big decision like finding just the right clock for the fireplace mantel and serene landscapes to hang on the walls. But then why would a rough, tough soldier care about any of that? He'd also admitted how much he worked. Why would a comfortable home even be high on his priority list? All he essentially needed was a place to park.

Which made her sad. Not for her, but for his son.

A survey of the kitchen showed Calder was right about her needing to go to the store. Unless she and Quinn wanted to eat baby-food peaches, carrots or protein shakes for breakfast, lunch and dinner, the day's first priority was a trip to the store.

Noting the blender on the counter, Pandora decided no more bland, premade fare for her tiny charge. "You're going gourmet, cutie."

Quinn giggled when she landed a playful poke to his belly.

At the restaurant where she used to work after first getting her life back on track, she'd struck up a fast friendship with the chef. Huge, funny and French, in his laughable English he'd taught her to prepare most everything on the menu and a few items that weren't. He'd been the only kind father figure she'd ever had, and his sudden heart attack had almost once again thrown her off course. All she remembered of her own dad was him constantly beating the crap out of her mom, occasionally taking a turn on her, then one day never coming home. Pandora would've thought her mom would be happy he was gone, but she'd suffered a meltdown—dying of an overdose near her forty-third birthday. Pandora, sixteen at the time, missed her, but for as long as she could remember, she'd virtually raised herself, doing her schoolwork as well as all the cooking and household chores, so the loss hadn't come as any great shock. The distant aunt who'd taken official custody of her was all too happy for Pandora to remain self-sufficient. The ratty apartment's rent and utilities were covered by her mom's social security check. Pandora's other needs were met through charity or after-school jobs.

The fact that her own mother had fallen apart should've served as the fire in her belly to make a better life for herself, but through counseling, Pandora now realized she'd fallen into the same abusive spiral.

Catching herself staring out the kitchen window, she said to the baby, "What do you think about from now on just focusing on our awesome future?"

He blew a raspberry in agreement.

"We have a lot to do. Not only is grocery shopping on our list, but I'll need you to help me find a really pretty comforter and all the trimmings."

Blue eyes wide, he hung on to her every singsong word.

"I know you're a boy and probably don't think a whole lot about things being pretty, but if you'd spent the past few years living where I have, you'd want to be surrounded by pretty things, too."

Quinn babbled happily in response.

Turned out Calder's car was as dreamy as his home. Her whole life, the closest she'd ever come to driving a new car had been when the mother of the children she used to work for had gotten a Lexus for her birthday and Pandora and the girls rode in the backseat on their way to a country-club party.

The Land Rover's powerful engine didn't sputter when she stopped for red lights and the tan leather upholstery smelled as good as it looked. In the rearview mirror, she regularly peeked at Quinn, all snug and smiley in his safety seat, gnawing on a rattle. Even he seemed to enjoy the ride.

The two of them made a few stops to find just the right floral bed set and fluffy yellow towels to match. Purchasing the items took nearly all her cash, but it was worth it.

With her purchases stashed in the back, she and Quinn headed to the grocery store.

Pandora had never bought so much food at once. Milk and eggs. Fruits, meats and veggies. When Calder said they were low on groceries, he hadn't been kidding. While standing at the checkout, the total felt uncomfortably large. Her pulse raced and her palms were damp. Would the card Calder had given her even work?

The youngish female clerk asked, "May I see your ID?"

"Um, sure, but I'm a nanny and this is my boss's card." With Quinn fussing in his carrier, Pandora fished through her purse for her driver's license.

"Sorry." The woman returned Calder's card to Pandora. "I'm not allowed to accept any credit card without matching ID."

"Please," Pandora begged. "It's way past time for my baby to have his lunch, and—"

"You just said he's not yours?"

"Well, yeah, but you know what I mean. Can we ask a manager?"

"Don't you have an alternate form of payment?"

"No." As this was the only open checkout lane, a line had formed behind her. With nothing else to do, people started to stare.

"Is there a problem?" the middle-aged manager asked.

Pandora explained her situation.

Quinn's fussing morphed to crying.

"Please." She took him from his carrier, jiggling him on her hip.

"Look, I'm sorry." The manager voided her sale. "You seem like a nice lady, but corporate's cracking down on checking ID for all credit-card sales. There's a lot of fraud in this area and if your card turns out to be stolen, I'm losing my job. Can you get in touch with your boss? Have him come down here to show his ID? Then I'll set you up an account and next time you shop, this won't be a problem."

Pandora eyed her cart. It'd taken over an hour to carefully make her selections. Would Calder be upset if she called his cell?

With Quinn crying harder than ever, she took a deep breath and dialed the store's office phone.

"Sorry…" Calder hustled toward Pandora and Quinn. With a loaded shopping cart alongside her, she'd parked herself on a bench in front of the store manager's office. "I'm an idiot for not seeing this contingency."

"You're not angry?" As if she'd worried about his reaction, her shoulders sagged in relief. "Because I'm sorry I even had to call. But the baby's hungry and I didn't know what else to do."

When Quinn fussed, she hugged him closer, smoothing her hand up and down his back.

"How could I be upset with you when this was my fault? Should've thought this through."

After getting Pandora squared away with the manager to use his card, Calder purchased the groceries, then pushed the cart, following the nanny and his son to the car. He had a hard time not staring at her cute behind because she wore the hell out of her white shorts.

She turned around and said, "Let me get Quinn settled in his safety seat, then I'll unload everything. You get back to work."

"I'm not in a hurry." He already had the back popped open and had placed the gallon of milk and two bulging sacks inside.

"Still…" Finished with Quinn, she fussed with her hands. "This is my job."

Ah, this was some kind of boss issue. "Look, Pandora, technically I might be in charge, but realistically…?" He laughed. "You're the one with all the answers. I might place explosives on moving subs, but navigating the baby aisle in the supermarket is *way* over my head. I never know what kind of milk to buy, and baby food blows my mind. That makes us a team, okay?"

Smiling, she pushed up her glasses and nodded. "At least let me help."

When she brushed past, their forearms grazed and he caught a whiff of her floral-scented hair. Maybe it'd been too long since he'd been with a woman, or maybe he was just appreciative to finally have some help with Quinn—either way, being near her made him feel extra alert. Not so much an attraction as an appreciation. Curiosity, even, to discover more about what made her tick. None of which made sense, considering he barely knew her. But there it was all the same.

A minute later, they'd finished loading his SUV. "I'll follow you home to carry everything in."

"Really, I've got this," she assured him.

But because he'd been raised to always carry in the groceries, he insisted.

DURING THE SHORT DRIVE to Calder's house, relief shimmered through Pandora. Not only had he not been angered by having to interrupt his day to help her, but he'd been downright gallant. And now, offering to help her unload? Amazing. Her ex had declared anything to do with groceries *women's work.*

Once parked in the garage, she took Quinn while Calder handled her purchases.

In the house, she placed the still-fussing baby in his high chair, dampened a paper towel with warm water, then washed his little hands and hers. "Hold on a minute, pumpkin, and we'll get that hungry tummy filled."

She rummaged in the bags Calder had already piled on the counter. Spotting the one item she needed, she removed a box of teething biscuits and handed a cookie to Quinn.

For the longest time, he stared at the biscuit, inspecting it as if he was unsure what to do. When his next logical step was to put it in his mouth, he grinned, oblivious to the drool dripping from his gummy smile.

She wiped his chin with a fresh dishrag before fishing for one of the bibs she'd bought at the store. With it securely fastened to the enthusiastic eater, she set about putting away the groceries and making lunch.

"That's everything." Calder set the last of the bags on the kitchen table. Sitting in the chair next to his son, he asked, "What're you eating, bud?"

Quinn gurgled and waved his hands in the air. *"Bah!"*

"Really?" he teased his son. "Sounds good."

"It's a teething biscuit," Pandora explained. "Soothes his gums. Plus, buys me time to fix him a proper lunch."

"Ah...." Calder nodded. "How'd you learn about babies?"

For a moment she froze, then slipped into autoresponse mode, glad for the distraction of putting veggies in the fridge. "Mostly classes and on-the-job training. This is my first full-time position with infant care, but I've worked part-time for three other families. Little Jonah, an eleven-month-old, was my biggest challenge. He was a jumper. That baby was nearly the death of me. He'd try escaping his changing table, crib, playpen. Can't imagine the trouble he's going to cause his future teachers."

Calder laughed.

Inside, she felt the stirrings of guilt. More and more, he seemed like a great guy. She wished she could've just told him about Julia, but that would only raise more questions—some of which she may not have been able to answer. As Natalie reminded her, she was entitled to her private life. Her only job requirement was giving expert care to Quinn.

"No kidding. I hope Quinn doesn't try to pull that kind of stunt," Calder said, still chuckling.

While putting pork chops, chicken and beef in the freezer, she said, "I'm making Quinn pureed peas for lunch. Would you like the grown-up version with a grilled chicken breast?"

His grin did funny things to her stomach. "Thanks for the offer, but I had lunch back on base. Speaking of which..."

He stood, then kissed the top of Quinn's head. "Guess I'd better head back."

Pandora understood Calder's work was important, but once he was gone she struggled with the oddest sensation. Something akin to clouds blocking the sun.

ALL AFTERNOON, stuck in a stuffy classroom, Calder found his mind drifting to his brief time with Pandora and Quinn. There was so much he needed to learn about his son, but considering how Calder had come to be a father, he'd had a hell of a time adjusting. Sure, he'd read a few baby books, and the first week, his mom had come from North Carolina to help him through the initial crisis, but there were still times he wondered what had happened to his life.

Opening his apartment door to find a wailing, six-month-old baby blocking the way had been a shocker, to put it mildly. Quinn had been bundled in a beaten-up carrier, *talking* to his pinkie finger.

Since then, everything felt upside down. Calder always seemed to be rushing to catch up. Temporary sitters and day care never seemed to work out and, until finding the agency that had provided him with Pandora, he'd feared maybe having to take an extended leave until his kid started school.

Calm, capable Pandora struck him as an oasis in his child-care desert.

Tonight, instead of rushing around trying to figure out formula ratios and how to scrub Quinn without getting soap in his eyes, Calder figured that thanks to the new nanny, he was back to business as usual.

He'd grab a beer with Mason, Heath and Cooper—maybe even chat up a hot blonde.

Four hours later, Calder shared a table at a favorite SEAL hangout, Tipsea's, with his boys. "This is the life, huh, guys?"

Mason ate a pretzel. "I don't know. At lunch, when Garrett

was showing around all his family pics... Made me wonder if we're missing something, but then gazing out on tonight's sea of available beauties, I'm thinking I like my current life just fine. Can I get an amen?"

Calder and Mason clinked longneck brews.

At the opposite end of the table, Cooper raised his beer.

"You three keep living the dream..." Heath fished in a pocket of his camo fatigues. "But it's time for me to move on. Lookee what I bought for Patricia's birthday." He withdrew a black velvet box, flipped open the lid to display a decent-size rock.

"Whoa—you don't mean *move on* as in leaving the SEALs, do you?"

Heath almost choked on his beer. "Oh, hell, no. Just that she means the world to me and I want her to be my wife. We all saw the drama Deacon, Garrett and Tristan went through in their love lives, and I don't need it. She's the woman for me. Done. End of story."

"Good for you, man." Mason patted his back. "I felt that way once." He shook his head and laughed. "Good thing I came to my senses."

Calder laughed his ass off.

Heath flipped them both the bird. "Yuk it up. I'm gonna be the one sleeping on clean sheets every night that I'm home with a good meal in my belly and a nice, soft woman to hold."

"Should we check this guy for fever?" Cooper asked.

"Oh—I've got one." After pushing back his chair, Heath stood. "It's called Patricia Fever. I'm going home to her right now. You idiots are just jealous."

After lover boy took his leave, Calder ordered a burger. Once the waitress left, he said to his friends, "We should stage an intervention. Clearly, Hopper's traveling down a dangerous path."

"No kidding," Mason said.

Calder's dad loved the ladies, but he had this old-fashioned thing about marrying them before sleeping with them. He was now on his sixth wife, which Calder saw as ridiculous. Though his mom had long since happily remarried and Calder viewed his stepdad as a great guy, he still wanted nothing to do with the institution of marriage. To his way of thinking, marriage only kept good men down. Calder enjoyed women too much to ever settle for one. And truthfully—he winked at a saucy redhead—as much as the ladies seemed to enjoy him, it'd be a damn shame to forever take himself off the market. Vowing to remain available was his gift to womankind.

At least that's what he told himself, and anyone else who cared to ask why he was still single. In the dark of night, Calder suspected the real reason, but no way was he ever acknowledging the fact.

He, Mason and Cooper drank in silence for a while, staring out at the crowded dance floor. It was Eighties Night and Duran Duran blared over the sound system about hungry wolves.

Mason was first to break the conversational silence. "I've bitched about Melissa so much, you guys could probably recite my story for me. But in all these years, you two have never told yours."

Calder said, "That's because I don't have one."

Cooper tipped his cowboy hat. "Same here."

Mason twisted to face them. "You're telling me neither of you have ever been serious with a member of the fairer sex?"

"Nope," Cooper said. "Damn proud of it."

"Amen, brother." Calder and Cooper clinked beers.

Mason whistled. "You two are a rare, fortunate breed."

Calder grinned. "We know."

Only after downing his burger and taking a spin on the dance floor with not one blonde but three, Calder spotted a brunette who reminded him of the new nanny. His stomach lurched upon the realization that despite all his bragging, he'd enjoyed sharing a conversation with her in his kitchen, watching his boy chow down on his cookie, more than he had spending the past three hours in this bar.

PANDORA JUMPED WHEN the front door opened and in walked Calder. Almost nine, with Quinn long since tucked in for the night, she'd been alone for so long that the house almost felt as if it were her own.

"What's going on?" he asked, opening the entry-hall closet to set his motorcycle helmet on the top shelf.

"Not much. You?"

He sat in the armchair adjacent to the sofa. Was it her imagination or did he smell like a bar?

Though it was none of her business where he'd been, she asked, "Tired? You worked late." Early in her recovery, the faint trace of booze on his breath would've had her craving a drink. Now realizing how much those drinks had ultimately cost in regard to her daughter…? She was content to stick with sweet tea.

He shrugged. "I'm good. Workwise, it was a pretty slow day, so afterward, me and a few friends stopped off for a burger and beer. I chilled there for a while to be sure I was sober enough to drive."

She nodded.

"Quinn all right?"

"Perfect."

The house's silence that had only a few minutes earlier been comforting now served as a reminder of just how awkward her new position may be. She'd never stayed with a family before and she hadn't thought about the situation from the perspective that for all practical purposes, she now lived with this man.

Drip, drip, drip went the kitchen sink.

Outside, the neighbor's dog barked.

"Well…" Calder leaned forward, resting his elbows on his knees. "Since we're probably both thinking it, I'm going to come right out and say it—this is weird."

She exhaled with relief. "You're feeling it, too?"

"No offense, but the way you're sitting there all prim and proper like my mom, I'm afraid you're going to ground me for missing curfew."

She laughed. "Trust me, I'm the last person who'd judge." Although if she were in his position, she wouldn't waste so much as a second away from his son. She'd learned the hard way what it was like when you weren't able to see your child. The pain was indescribable.

"Now that we've got that dealt with—" he stood, tugging his T-shirt over his head "—I'm gonna grab a quick shower, then study a new manual."

"Um, sure." Her cheeks blazed. Faced yet again with his muscled-up chest, she was grateful he retreated to his room. The part of her craving adult conversation realized Calder's vanishing act was for the best.

He was her boss.

Not her friend—certainly not anyone whose bare chest she should be appraising.

Chapter Three

"Since you're still up, there's something I want to run past you."

An hour had gone by since they'd last talked, but judging by the way Pandora jumped when Calder entered the room, she'd been deeply absorbed in a parenting book.

"Scintillating?" he teased, running his hand over his bare chest.

When she glanced up at him, her cheeks reddened. "Um, not really. Just researching the proper way to introduce Quinn to more solid foods."

He nodded, fighting a flash of guilt for not having read the book he'd bought months earlier. "Last time I talked to my mom, she mentioned that."

"Oh?" Pandora's red cheeks fairly glowed. Ducking behind her book, she added, "That's nice."

What was her problem?

The air-conditioning kicked on, chilling what moisture still clung to his chest from the shower. Then it dawned on him—prim-and-proper Wonder Nanny didn't like him not wearing a shirt. She'd be the first woman in history who disapproved of his eight-pack, but as her employer, he supposed professional courtesy dictated he be fully dressed. Ducking into his room, he grabbed a clean T-shirt from an unfolded basket of laundry. After tugging it over his head, he returned to the living room. "I know I told you I didn't want to talk about Quinn's mother until I had a few beers in my system, but I guess since you're now his primary caregiver, you need to know why I'm not the sharpest tool in the shed when it comes to parenting."

"I've seen worse." She sipped from her iced tea.

"Not sure if that's good or bad."

"Good," she assured.

He struggled for the right place to start. "Until a couple months ago, I didn't know Quinn existed. Back then, I shared an apartment with friends and one morning I opened the door to find Quinn in his carrier. A Post-it attached to the handle pretty much said his mom quit and now it was my turn to be his parent."

Hands over her mouth, Pandora's striking green eyes shone with unshed tears. "That's crazy. Where is she now? What if something had happened to him while he was alone? You don't even know anything about his medical records."

"Yeah," he said with a sarcastic chuckle, "tell me about it. I took him to a pediatrician and he seems healthy. Had a DNA test run and sure enough, he's mine. Only—and I'm not proud of this—I don't have a clue who his mom could be."

"You haven't heard from her? How could she just leave her child without at least reassuring herself that he's okay? What if you hadn't even been home, but off on one of your missions?"

"Valid questions." Running his hand over his whisker-stubbled jaw, Calder said, "I have to assume she knew my car, and when she saw it parked out front, guessed I was home. Still, the whole thing's thrown me off my game. I've been asking tons of questions from everyone I know who has a kid. Bought this house so Quinn would have a backyard. Tonight was the first time I've been out with my friends in what feels like forever."

"Was it as fun as you've no doubt imagined?"

Leaning back in his chair, he stared at the ceiling. "It was all right." What he wouldn't admit was that his good time had been partially ruined by mental images of her. Of wondering what she and Quinn were doing. Was the little guy playing with his plastic boats in the bath? All of which made no sense, considering how grateful he'd been to hand over his kid to a practical stranger.

"Sorry. Hopefully, now that I'm here, you can get back to your old routine."

"Yeah. That'd be good." But would it? And now that Calder had Quinn, was it even possible to revert to the way his life used to be? Before having a kid, he'd had no worries beyond making it to duty on time. Now he had a constant streaming checklist of diapers and baby food and formula. Granted, all of that was now Pandora's domain, but what kind of dad would he be to just let her take over Quinn's parenting in full?

"You ever worry about what you'll do if Quinn's mother suddenly shows up, wanting to take him back?"

"Thought's crossed my mind." In those first rough days, he'd found himself praying for just such a scenario. But as time went on, he'd gotten angry. Calder might not be the best dad, but he sure as hell would never leave his kid on a doorstep. "At this point, I doubt any judge would grant custody to a mother who pulled this kind of stunt. I mean, what kind of woman abandons her child?"

"I don't know…." Was it his imagination, or had she paled?

As much as Pandora cherished Calder's quiet home during her first day, she struggled falling asleep in the still of night. After hours of fitful tossing and turning, she was relieved to hear Quinn cry over the baby monitor.

She went to him, scooping him from his crib for a quick diaper change before making him a bottle. By this age, she was surprised he wasn't sleeping through the night, but after what Calder told her, she suspected the little guy was waking not from hunger, but an innate need for reassurance that while he'd slept, his world hadn't once again fallen apart.

In the kitchen, Quinn on her hip, she said to the sleepy boy, "When your dad told me your mom abandoned you, I felt sad. But then I felt guilty. By choosing to drink over raising my little girl, is that what I did to her?"

Quinn nuzzled his head against her neck. His warmth, the downy-soft feel of his hair, filled her with achy longing for her own child.

Soon, Julia. Soon.

Her next court date wasn't until spring, but that was okay. By then, she'd have saved even more money—enough to provide her daughter with the true home she'd always deserved.

Pandora turned on the overhead light, heated the formula and poured the liquid into Quinn's bottle. But as she tried to add water to the pan with one hand, it slipped, clanging Quinn into instant, startled tears.

"I'm sorry," she crooned, setting the bottle on the counter to free both her arms for soothing. "I didn't mean to scare you. It was just a loud noise. Nothing *really* scary." Like the nightmares she still had of the day her Julia had been taken.

"Everything all right?" Calder, wearing nothing but athletic shorts, hovered on the kitchen's threshold. As was beginning to be habit, her mouth went dry at just the sight of him and her pulse raced. At what point did her body get the memo that as her boss, not only was the man off limits, but she had no interest in romance—period? Her life's sole focus was regaining custody of her child.

"Fine," she murmured, wishing she wore more than a

flimsy, too-short nightgown. "Sorry we woke you. I dropped a pan, which scared this guy."

"Glad it was nothing major." He ambled toward the fridge. "Got anything good in here?"

"There's leftover meat loaf from dinner. If you'll take Quinn, I'll make you a sandwich."

He groaned. "I know making late-night snacks for me is hardly the job description I gave to your agency, but man, does that sound like a good trade."

Laughing, she handed him the baby, trying to ignore the almost electric awareness stemming from an act as simple as brushing against his hands and forearms. Even harder to ignore, though, was the heat radiating from his magnificent chest—and his smell. Manly soap mixed with faint sweat.

Reminding herself of the task at hand, she made quick work of assembling his meal while he sat at the table with Quinn. "Ketchup or mayo?"

"Gotta go with ketchup."

"Warm or cold?"

With another happy groan, he asked, "Woman, how has some lucky guy not snatched you up?"

If he only knew…. "Stick to the question at hand, sir."

"Fair enough." He failed to look remotely chastised. "I'm used to eating pretty near anything, anywhere, but since you asked, warm sounds off-the-chart good."

She nuked the sandwich. When the microwave dinged, she set his plate in front of him. "Be careful. It could be too hot."

"Thanks. If this tastes anywhere near as good as it smells, I might steal you away from Quinn to make you my personal chef."

Pandora held out her arms for the baby, steeling herself to disregard any physical pleasure stemming from the exchange. "Judging by what you've told me about your eating habits, sounds like he needs me more than you."

"Probably true."

When Calder took his first bite, Pandora realized she'd been holding her breath in anticipation of his verdict. It shouldn't matter whether or not he liked her silly sandwich, but it did.

Only when he smiled did she exhale. "All I can say is wow. If the mashed-up food you feed Quinn is half as good as this, he is one lucky kid."

Fairly glowing from Calder's compliment, Pandora had the feeling she was the lucky one.

After his latest bite, Calder glanced at her, then cocked his head. "You look different."

"I'm, um, not wearing my glasses. They're mainly for reading and driving. Long-distance stuff."

He nodded. "You look good—not that I mind glasses, just that…" He reddened. "I'm gonna finish my sandwich."

Mortification didn't come close to describing the emotion surging through Pandora. She looked *good?* What did that even mean? In manspeak, was that a step above ugly, yet beneath homely? Moreover, why did she care?

"So it's the middle of the night," Calder said to his friends during a break in day two of smart-bomb training. "I hear Quinn screaming, only once I find him in the kitchen with the new nanny, he's already settled down. And damn if she doesn't look pretty good in this skimpy naughty-nightie number. Her hair was all down and a little crazy and she'd even lost her glasses. Anyway, so next thing I know—"

Mason whistled. "You two put the baby to bed, then got busy?"

"Get your mind out of the gutter." Calder smacked the back of Mason's head with one of the wiring manuals they were supposed to be studying. "From there, she makes me a meat-loaf sandwich I swear was better than sex."

"Sounds to me like you're not doing it right." Heath high-fived Mason.

Calder shot them both dirty looks.

Cooper never stopped reading.

"All I'm saying is I think I found a keeper."

"Don't you mean Quinn found a keeper?" Deacon asked.

"Who asked you, married man?"

Finishing the last swig of his bottled water, Deacon shrugged. "Just pointing out that for a guy who hates female attachments, and considering this nanny's only been on the job twenty-four hours, you're sounding awfully content."

"What's wrong with that? As long as I keep things professional with Pandora, I can see this working out for a nice long time. I do what I want. Quinn's getting great care. It's a win-win for all involved."

Heath snorted. "What's the nanny getting out of it?"

Calder winked. "The pleasure of seeing me."

"IT'S A LITTLE BARE, but it has good bone structure." Natalie, in her official capacity as the owner of Earth Angels, the child-care agency Pandora worked for, finished her walk-through of Calder's home and set her clipboard on the kitchen counter. "I know it's only been one night, but how was it?"

"Good." Pandora held Quinn, waging a playful battle over who had control of her glasses. So far, the baby was winning.

"Care to elaborate?"

"It was very good. Awkward at first, but I guess that's to be expected. Did you know Quinn was literally left on Calder's doorstep? Calder's only had him a few months."

"Whoa." Natalie sat at the table. "Sure your new boss wasn't pulling your leg? He certainly didn't divulge any of that while filling out his paperwork. Sounds crazy."

"Tell me about it. Remember how when I first asked about

Quinn's mother, he put me off? I assumed they must've had a nasty divorce, but I never expected anything like this."

Quinn squirmed to be let down, so Pandora set him on the wood floor she'd cleaned earlier that morning.

"Luckily, Quinn doesn't show signs of abandonment issues."

"He did wake up around two last night. Seemed more interested in having a nice cuddle than a bottle."

"Poor thing…." Natalie shook her head, then sighed. "Well, I've got two more stops, then a mountain of paperwork back at the office, so I'd better go."

When she stood, Pandora gave her friend a hug. "Even though your stay was official, it was nice seeing you. We should do lunch."

"For sure. And didn't you have a visit with Julia last Saturday? How'd it go?"

"I wish. Her foster family rented a beach house, so we needed to postpone until this week."

Just thinking about seeing her daughter filled Pandora with anticipation, but also resentment. To her way of thinking, Julia should've been returned at least a year ago.

"I know that look," Natalie said with another quick hug. "Be patient. Before you know it, you'll be spending every night going over homework and driving to soccer practice."

Pandora crossed her arms. "From your lips to God's ears…."

"YOU'RE HOME EARLY."

In the entry hall, Calder shrugged. "A few guys were setting up a volleyball game down at the beach, but I wasn't feeling it. You two, on the other hand, look like you're having fun." Pandora sat on the floor with Quinn, building a block tower. When she placed the last block on top, he knocked the whole thing down, shrieking and laughing with delight. In the short time he'd had his son, Calder had never seen him this happy, which produced a mixed bag of emotions. Part of him was thrilled with Quinn's smile, but another side of him regretted not having been able to produce the same results.

Pandora grinned up at him. "It's looking more and more like your son is destined to become Master of the Universe."

"Sounds like a noble calling." That was it. The last of anything witty he had to say. Pandora and Quinn were back to their two-person game and Calder stood there like an oaf, not sure what to do with his hands.

Why hadn't he gone to the beach with his friends?

He knew why. Guilt had damn near eaten him alive. The whole point of hiring a nanny—aside from caring for Quinn—was so Calder could get back some semblance of his former life. So why did he feel like a louse each time he tried to do just that?

She glanced his way. "Want to take over for me? I should probably start dinner."

"Sure." Inspiration struck. "But would you rather pack up the kiddo and head down to the beach to hang with my team? They're cooking out."

"Will there be a lot of drinking?" Of all the questions she might have asked, that wasn't one he'd expected.

"Maybe beer. But it's a *school* night, so if you're worried about Quinn being around a bunch of drunk guys, I doubt anyone's going to get hammered."

She fiddled with her messy ponytail. "I don't even own a bathing suit."

"You don't have to go in the water. Come on, it'll be fun." And it sure as hell beat sitting around here, trying to drum up something clever to say.

"I don't know...." The way she worried her lower lip, drawing it into her mouth so a sliver of her teeth showed, struck him as sexy.

"Come on. Think of it as an official duty. I'm making you go, since I'd like to be with Quinn *and* my friends. More important, if you're not there, who'll hold the baby while I play?"

She sighed, but pushed to her feet. "Give me a sec to change into shorts and get gear and a bottle for Quinn."

"WHOA, THIS A MIRAGE?"

"Lay off, Hopper," Calder said to one of the guys they'd just approached. Feeling awkward around more of the hulking SEALs who were similar in stature to her boss, Pandora welcomed the distraction of Quinn making his usual play for her glasses.

Calder made introductions and everyone seemed nice, but once the volleyball game started and she and Quinn were relegated to the sidelines to sit with a girlfriend of one of the SEALs, Pandora felt like the proverbial third wheel.

Which shouldn't have mattered.

It wasn't as if she and Calder were even friends, so why had a twinge of disappointment lodged in her belly over the fact that for all practical purposes, she might as well be invisible? It was ridiculous.

Though she'd worked for her last family over a year, she could count on one hand the number of times she'd spoken to the girls' father. What was it about this position that should be any different?

Calder's team scored and he high-fived the other guys.

As was starting to be an alarming trend, he'd taken off his shirt. His friends had also lost theirs. The level of male perfection, highlighted in the sun's early-evening glow was undeniably heady. Yet, at the same time, it left Pandora feeling all the more lonely. It was obvious these men were a tight family unit.

The woman beside Pandora constantly cheered on her man.

Even Quinn unearthed something more interesting than her. His expression turned intense while studying driftwood he'd found in the sand.

Pandora may have grown a lot over the years, but sadly, without Julia, she was still on her own, yet craving more. Once and for all, she wanted to be part of a real family. But she knew better than to think she'd find that in a man like Calder. Even if they'd met under different circumstances, what would he want with her? They came from opposite worlds. He was college educated, as she'd seen from the framed diploma he'd stacked along with other yet-to-be-hung pictures in the linen closet.

Had he known Quinn's mom carried his child, would he have married her? What qualities would he find attractive enough in a woman to make him want to stick around?

Chapter Four

"I can't get used to the idea of Calder being a dad."

Pandora glanced up from feeding Quinn his bottle to find a pretty redhead sitting beside her. They'd finished grilling hot dogs and the guys had returned to their game.

"I'm Patricia, by the way."

"Pandora. Nice to meet you." She shook her new friend's hand.

The baby grunted at the interruption in his bottle, but soon enough was back to contentedly downing his meal.

The team playing opposite Calder's spiked a ball deep into their territory, and the men erupted into a slew of good-natured name-calling—further startling the baby.

"Rowdy bunch, huh?" Patricia ran her hand along Quinn's downy hair while Pandora comforted him.

"I've seen worse." No way was Pandora prepared to share the number of drug-induced bar fights she'd witnessed. During her blackest moments, when alcohol had no longer been enough, she'd done and seen things that to this day made her deeply ashamed. She may have technically paid for her crimes, but that didn't mean her soul had been cleared from all wrongdoing.

"My guy's Heath—that big lug to Calder's right. If you're like me, it'll take forever to get everyone's names straight."

"I can see why." Quinn had finished his bottle, so Pandora

tucked it into his diaper bag, trading it for a burping cloth she positioned over her left shoulder. She eased the fussy baby upright for burping and soon enough, despite the noise, he struggled to keep his eyes open.

"I can't wait to have kids." Patricia gazed longingly toward Quinn. "My birthday's Sunday and rumor has it, Heath's finally popping the question. We plan to get started on our family right away."

"Want to hold him?" Pandora offered her the baby.

"Yes, please." The switch was awkward and filled with laughing.

"Mmm…" Cradling Quinn, Patricia closed her eyes and smiled. "He's amazing. When Heath told me the story of how this cutie was abandoned, it still makes me mad. Like, seriously? Who does such a thing? That woman was the world's worst mother. Probably strung out on booze or worse."

"No doubt." A knot formed at the back of Pandora's throat. No matter how hard she swallowed, it refused to budge. Would it always be this tough? Remembering the woman she used to be? She had no right judging Quinn's mom, as she'd once been every bit as bad.

"Quinn smells so good. I come from a large family, but since I was the baby, I never got to play with a real live one till my nieces and nephews started coming."

"Must've been amazing," Pandora said, "growing up in a big, loving family."

"Mostly it was." She laughed. "Although, I still cringe when I think of sharing a bathroom with so many people."

Patricia's statement had been innocent enough, but brought still more bad memories of the halfway house where Pandora had spent the past couple years. It had sure beaten living on the streets, but in some ways it had been harder. So many people and rules. So many reminders of how close she'd come to losing it all.

Reminding herself those days were finally behind her, Pandora forced a smile. "How long have you and Heath been together?"

"Two excruciatingly long years." Cradling Quinn, her smile turned wistful. "It's hard enough being with a SEAL—you never know when they're coming or going. Only the wives have any glimmer of real knowledge as to what's going on. We lowly girlfriends never know anything."

"Oh—I'm not Calder's girlfriend," Pandora said quickly. "Just Quinn's nanny."

"Sorry. I forgot. We don't see many of those. How long have you been with him?"

Pandora laughed. "Actually, this is only my second night. So far, so good."

Quinn started to fuss.

"Spoke too soon?" Pandora didn't mind when Patricia returned Quinn to her waiting arms. She'd only been with the infant a short while, but she'd already learned to decipher his basic cries. Hunger. Dirty diaper. Sleepy. Babies were relatively simple to figure out.

Quinn's father, on the other hand…

In the setting sun's orange glow, Pandora made the mistake of looking up to find Calder in all his bare-chested glory rising up to spike the ball. He struck her as powerful and in control—not at all the same man she'd encountered when Quinn had been choking. Assuming Calder worked with the same efficiency in his capacity as a SEAL as he did on the volleyball court, what did that say about his parenting skills? The fact that the only time he appeared truly happy and at peace was when he wasn't caring for his son.

Not that Pandora was judging. Just curious to discover more about him.

Calder's team won, but by the time they'd defended their

victory by besting their challengers in a two-out-of-three series, the sunset's glow had long since faded to dark.

Quinn slept soundly against her, and since Patricia and
her soon-to-be fiancé had skipped out a while back, Pandora
had spent the past hour staring out at the dark surf. She grew
up on the wrong side of the tracks in small-town Virginia,
so her only memories of visiting the beach were imagined.
Fourth of Julys she'd dreamed of watching fireworks. Running barefoot in the sand with a whole pack of sparklers all
for herself. Birthdays she'd envisioned with friends splash-
ing with her in the surf and building sand castles. In her rich
fantasy life, she'd even had mermaid-themed cupcakes and
balloons.

Back to reality, it was hard to believe she'd finally met her
lifelong dream of seeing the Atlantic. The faint, briny-scented
breeze and the rhythmic crashing of the waves proved hyp-
notic, making her think of a life that might've been. Regret
upon regret for not at least giving her own daughter the happiness she deserved.

"Ready?" Calder asked beside her, jolting her to the present.

"Ah, sure." It took her a few seconds to regain her composure. But then her boss took Quinn, inadvertently brushing
her breasts in the trade-off. Only, the invasion of her personal
space didn't feel like an invasion at all. More like the kind of
natural thing that happens between a man and woman sharing a relationship and raising a child.

But they didn't share any of that. For all practical purposes, they were strangers.

"Sorry." He held out his hand to help her to her feet.

"It's okay." She accepted his help, but soon regretted the
decision. When their fingers touched, the usual sparks were
there tenfold, making her unsure about her next move. Had
he felt it, too?

If so, he showed no indication. All polite business, he fastened Quinn into his carrier, then hefted the baby and diaper bag. "That everything?"

"Uh-huh." Except for the irrational part of her wondering what it would be like to have a real connection with a man as decent as Calder.

"THIS WAS GOOD." Over the years, Calder had had many women in his passenger seat, but none who set him on edge quite like Pandora. Why, he didn't know, but he took her prim posture and pressed-lip silence to mean he'd done something wrong. Knowing full well he hadn't and was just being paranoid, he decided to make a game out of coaxing the woman to speak. "You and Quinn have fun?"

"We did. The beach is always a treat."

"Yeah?" He glanced her way to find her fogging her glasses, then wiping them on a tissue she'd drawn from her purse. "What was your favorite thing about spending time at the shore?"

She slowly exhaled. "I liked the smell. The waves sounded just like I've always imagined."

"Wait." Stopped at a red light, he turned to her. "You mean to tell me tonight was your first trek to the beach?"

"Embarrassing, right?"

After checking the rearview mirror to ensure there were no other cars around, Calder made a U-turn.

"What're you doing?"

"Well, hell, woman." He shot her a sideways grin. "You're a bona fide Atlantic virgin—an elusive and mystical creature, to be sure."

"Sure you weren't spiking your cola?"

"Nope." He made a left, aiming the SUV back to where they'd just come from. "We're on a mission."

"To do what?"

"Something we would've done earlier if I'd known what a momentous occasion this was. We need to get those toes of yours in the water."

"Calder, you're being silly." She glanced to the backseat. "It's already late and Quinn's covered in sand. He'll need a quick bath before bed and I'll need to clean his carrier."

"So? It's not like you have to be at a desk bright and early."

"But you no doubt do."

"Haven't you learned it's impolite to argue with your boss?"

He took her shy smile to mean he'd broken at least a small part of her reserve. "Please don't take this the wrong way, but are you mentally stable enough to protect our country?"

For a split second, he thought she was serious, but then he caught her wink and burst out laughing. "You almost had me."

"You've got to admit this whole notion of sticking my toes in the water sounds a bit off the deep end."

Now he winked. "I'm not suggesting you go deep, Ms. Moore. Merely dip your toes in the shallow end. It's a serious rite of passage."

"It's a rite of passage that can wait. Quinn's comfort and needs come first."

"In case you haven't noticed—" he veered into the parking spot they'd vacated only ten minutes earlier "—Quinn is out. I don't think he'll mind the slight detour."

After having a look for herself, she said, "You've got me there." In the glow of the dash lights, her expression morphed from doubt to wary acceptance to anticipation. "But is this really prudent?"

He laughed. "Does it matter? Come on." He almost held out his hand to her, but then thought better of it. He wanted to have a little fun, but not present the image of being interested in *that way.* "Last one in is a rotten egg!"

"Who's getting Quinn?"

"Me, so you'd better hustle."

Pandora kicked off her sandals and ran and ran, laughing until she reached the shore. The water was cold but refreshing and unexpected and hit her as an affirmation her life was finally on the right track. Granted, her current actions may not be dignified, but for at least a few minutes that was okay. She could let her guard down a smidge—just not too much.

Had she denied herself the beach's simple pleasures for so long because she hadn't felt good enough? Like only clean, wholesome people visit such enchanted places?

"How is it?" Calder asked from behind her. Quinn slept cradled against him.

"Wonderful," she admitted. And honestly, if she hadn't had to work so hard to earn her way to this spot, this very moment in time, she might not have appreciated it for the miracle it truly was. As soon as she regained custody of Julia, a trip to the beach was in order.

"If you don't mind my asking," he said above the surf that pounded louder than it had earlier, "how's it even possible you've lived around here yet have never been to the shore?"

"Just one of those things." Though her gut told her she could probably trust him with the truth, her head warned the less he knew about her past, the better off they'd both be.

The nighttime breeze had considerably cooled the air.

Pandora said, "We should get back to the car."

"What's your hurry?"

"I-it's cold." At first, she'd been exhilarated by their fun, but now she was somewhat ashamed. Almost as if being in such a clean, family-friendly place might mark her a fraud. But was she? She'd worked hard to get to the healthy emotional zone in which she now resided. Didn't that count for something?

She wiped tears from her cheeks, glad for the darkness so Calder wouldn't see.

"You okay?"

"Sure." She hoped her exaggerated nod read as convincing.

"It's all right, you know."

"Wh-what?"

"If the sight of moonlight on the ocean moves you." He reached his hand toward her, brushing first one tear-stained cheek, then the other with the pad of his thumb.

His touch affected her far more deeply than it should have. Embarrassed, she looked away. "I'm fine—the wind blew sand in my eyes."

"Locational hazard…." His soft tone told her he knew she was lying. The fact both mortified her and filled her with hope he'd never guess just how much their shared moment had truly meant. Whatever their future, she'd always associate him with the moment she realized her efforts really were finally making a difference. Soon, she'd not only have her daughter returned, but her dignity.

MIDWAY THROUGH CHANGING Quinn's diaper at five-thirty the next morning, Calder was startled by Pandora's appearance at his side. Apparently she'd felt as awkward about her choice of late-night attire at their last meeting as he had. Not that he hadn't been appreciative of her miles of creamy skin, but her current chaste, white cotton pj's were infinitely less seductive.

"What're you doing up?" he asked. "We were trying to be extra quiet to let you sleep."

"That's nice of you," she said as she passed the wipes, "but my job description is to care for Quinn in order to allow you more rest."

"I had to be up anyway. Got a text we're doing early drills." After wiping down his son, Calder tossed the soiled diaper in the trash, then reached for a fresh one.

"Put cream on his bottom."

"What cream?"

She handed him a tube. "Last time I changed him, I noticed he looked a little chafed. No biggie. Just something to keep an eye on."

"Sure." Calder flipped open the lid. "How much?"

"A dime."

"Did you grab this stuff at the store?"

"Uh-huh." She stood near enough for him to feel her heat. Not a good thing, considering he hadn't been as smart as her and still slept in just boxers. "Want me to finish up with him so you can grab a shower?"

"Trying to get rid of me?" He was only half teasing. Ever since the beach, she'd been quiet. He'd meant for their outing to be fun, but he couldn't help but wonder what'd brought on her tears. He'd wanted to ask her on the drive home, and again while they'd bathed Quinn, but the timing hadn't seemed right. Besides, were her tears even his business?

"No." Her smile seemed genuine. "Just trying to be helpful."

"Thanks." The more time he shared with Pandora, the more confused he grew. When it came to the fairer sex, he excelled at the short game. One or two nights—tops. Mornings could be tricky, so he avoided them like brussels sprouts. So here he was on his second morning with the nanny and despite the fact they'd barely even spoken, let alone had sex, he honestly wasn't sure how many more he could take. Something about her had him all riled up and flustered—in his line of work, never a good thing.

With Quinn tucked back into his snap-bottom T-shirt, Pandora scooped him up and cradled him against her.

His son looked happy, and that fact calmed Calder's choppy nerves. Truly, he needed to chill. Pandora was the nanny. Nothing more. No need to rely on his usual shtick, or

worry about spending too much time with one woman, because she wasn't his woman. If anything, he should treat her
like one of the guys. "Got anything going on this weekend?
Thought we might get back to the beach, only this time do it
up proper. More volleyball. Soggy sandwiches. It'll be great."

"Um…" She looked to the baby, out the window, to the
changing table—anywhere but him. "That sounds amazing,
but I have plans."

"Oh?" He'd placed her firmly in the friend zone, so why
did he feel shot down? It didn't happen often, which left him
needing answers. Only because he was her employer, no
matter how much he wanted to drill her about what she was
doing that could be more important than chilling with him
and his son—he knew damn well he couldn't. Shouldn't. It
would be a seriously needy move, and Calder never lacked
for female attention.

"Rain check? I've never been on a picnic, so…" As her
words trailed off, so did her eye contact. Interesting. What
would the nanny be doing on Saturday? Or should that *what*
be replaced by a *who?*

Chapter Five

Wednesday afternoon, the computers Calder's team had been using to study the latest Afghanistan satellite-photo-intelligence models were down. Cooper and Heath used the opportunity to nap. Calder and Mason had just finished a five-mile run and sat on a bench, soaking in rays.

"Damn nice day," Mason said. "Reminds me why I left Alaska."

Calder had tilted his head back and closed his eyes. He opened them to glance sideways at his friend. "Thought you bolted because of Melissa."

"Well, that, too. But mainly because of the weather."

"Uh-huh. You've given me so much crap over the nanny, I'm shoveling it back your way."

Resting his arms behind his head, Mason said, "Whatever. Speaking of which, haven't heard much about her today. Everything all right?"

Calder sighed. "I guess it's going good. Both Quinn and the house are freakishly clean, and she's a great cook." That said, the beach rejection stung his manly pride. His rational side knew giving the matter a second thought was ridiculous. The part of him used to women falling for his SEAL charm still didn't get it. What had he done wrong? "Look, I shouldn't even mention this to you, but after the volleyball game, I found out Pandora had never been to the beach."

"What?" Mason scratched his head.

"I know, right? Anyway, I've been meaning to spend more time with the little guy, so I figured we'd do the whole day-at-the-shore thing with him on Saturday, only—"

Mason laughed. "She turned you down, didn't she?"

Lips pressed tight, Calder had never wished more he'd kept his big mouth shut.

Still laughing, Mason said, "Mr. Professional Working Relationship who yelled at us for asking if Pandora was a sex-kitten nanny broke his own rule, huh?"

"Forget it. Sorry I brought it up." Calder had honestly thought it would be a good idea to spend time with Quinn. The beach was always fun. The whole thing shouldn't have been a big deal.

Standing, Calder headed back to the building housing their classroom.

"Aw, come on...." Mason trailed after him. "Don't go getting your panties in a wad. I'm sure the nanny has a perfectly good reason for turning down your date."

"It wasn't a date," Calder snapped. "I don't like her that way. Wouldn't be right."

"Might not be right, but if she's hot and you two share tight quarters, what's your plan to keep things platonic?"

Calder tugged open the metal door, welcoming the rush of cool air. "Drop it, okay? I don't need a plan, because nothing's going to happen."

"Then why are you so pissy over her wanting an afternoon for herself?" Mason stopped off at a vending machine.

Though his friend asked a valid question, Calder didn't have an answer. If pressed, he suspected his true problem stemmed from the simple fact he was scared to death of once again being alone with his son.

CALDER RODE STRAIGHT home from the base only to find Quinn and Pandora heading down the block. He parked his bike in the garage, then hollered in their direction, "Wait up!"

After closing the door, he pocketed the opener, jogging to meet them.

"Hey." She veered the stroller against the sidewalk's edge to make room for him. "How was your day?"

He shrugged. Now that he'd caught up with the duo, he wasn't sure why he'd even tried. All smiles, Quinn kicked and made baby noises. Pandora had been smiling. However, since his arrival, she'd pressed her lips into a telling line of tension. "You two headed for the park?"

She nodded. "They have great baby swings—you know? The one's that are safety seats?"

"Guess I've never much noticed."

"Quinn loves them."

Another dig at Calder's parenting? Or lack thereof?

They walked the last two blocks in silence. The temperature was already cooling off with a hint of approaching autumn in the air. Even from their distance, the sounds of kids playing—laughing—rang clearly through the air. He couldn't remember ever having been that kid—fully carefree. Sure, after his mom had remarried, things settled down, but he'd been past the playground age.

Upon reaching the park, it struck Calder as surprisingly full. "There always this many people here?"

"It's a park. Most times, there's even more." Her sideways look, not to mention her pinched expression, didn't sit well with him. Yet again, he felt inept. He'd lived a few blocks from what was apparently a family mecca, yet it'd never even occurred to him it was anywhere he and Quinn might want to be.

"Sorry. I didn't know."

"It's not a big deal, Calder." She parked the stroller in front of the lone empty bench in a row of five. "Now that you're here, want to put Quinn in a swing?"

Visions of Quinn screaming whenever Calder tried cramming him into his car seat ran through his head. "No, thanks."

Pandora effortlessly plucked Quinn from his stroller to plop him into the rubber swing seat and strapped him in. As if the kid knew what came next, he giggled and kicked. The size of his drool-filled grin tugged at Calder's heart.

From Pandora's first small push, Quinn howled with laughter. He clapped his little hands and bounced and kicked. His eyes shone with what Calder could only describe as pure glee. Burning heat forced his eyes to close for a moment while at the same time he swallowed the knot at the back of his throat.

He'd never seen Quinn like this—truly happy. But now that he had, something in him clicked. Was this at least partially what parenting was about? Not just keeping your child fed and clean, but figuring out what produced adorable grins? Then earning them over and over again?

"You want to push?" Pandora stepped aside, urging Calder to give it a try.

"What if I push him too high? Is he going to fall out?"

Hands on her hips, she cocked her head. "Really?"

"Well…" He forced a deep breath. "Stranger things could happen."

Approaching the swing, Calder couldn't have said why, but his pulse raced and his palms began to sweat. He crouched to reach the little guy, then pushed just enough for Quinn to shriek all over again. "He's doing it!"

"You thought he wouldn't?" Pandora asked. "See? You're doing great. Now whenever I'm not around, you can bring him here on your own. Once he starts walking, he's going to love the rope bridge and slide."

Calder took one glance at the wood-planked bridge hanging between two roofed forts. "No way. Too dangerous."

Now Pandora was the one laughing. "If you think that's scary, wait till he gets his first bike."

AFTER YET ANOTHER delicious dinner, helping with Quinn's bath and tucking him in, Calder fired off a few emails, then tracked down Pandora in the laundry room, folding pint-size T-shirts. A few larger ones he recognized as his own were already stacked neatly beside his son's.

"Need help?"

"No, thank you. Almost done." The faint smile she cast over her shoulder made him almost as confused as he'd been that afternoon when he saw his son in the swing. Pandora was constantly doing things for him, but Calder never reciprocated. It was her job to care for Quinn, but she spoiled them both.

"You know I don't expect you to do my laundry."

"I don't mind. Besides, Quinn's whites barely took up half a load."

"Okay, well..." Suddenly tongue-tied in the cramped space, he crammed his hands in the pockets of his fatigues. "Thanks. You're a nice lady." *A nice lady?* Calder mentally smacked his forehead. What the hell kind of line was that?

Forehead furrowed, she half laughed. "Thanks. I think."

He covered his face with his hands. "Sorry. That sounded like I think you're eighty. Obviously, you're not." Her black yoga pants and pink T-shirt hugged her in all the right places—even her crooked ponytail enhanced her pretty glow.

"I hope not." Laughing again, she glanced down shyly before pushing up her glasses. "At eighty, I'm not sure I'll have the energy needed to chase after your son."

"Okay, well, whatever your age, I very much appreciate

all you've been doing—not only for Quinn, but me. You're an angel."

She turned from him to place the folded clothes into a basket. "I wouldn't go that far."

SATURDAY MORNING, Calder bumped into Pandora on her way out of her bedroom. "You smell good." The second the words left his mouth, he kicked himself for yet again having nothing smoother to say. The more he was around Pandora, the more he sounded like a mooning fourth grader. Now that the weekend had arrived and Pandora was obviously dolling herself up for someone, he was merely taking a healthy interest in her day's plans. Any good friend would, right? Only, were they even friends? To cover his confusion, he blurted, "Seeing someone special?"

Quinn sat in his walker, grinning and drooling while pressing a squeaky frog head. *"Rah gaa!"*

"Very." Was it his imagination, or had her green eyes grown brighter from the size of her smile?

Mom? Favorite uncle? Grandmother? *Boyfriend?* So what if she did have a boyfriend? In the week she'd worked for Calder, she'd proved herself to be not only an excellent caregiver for Quinn but a great housekeeper and cook. Calder had no complaints. He'd never even caught her on the phone. Which meant if she did have a boyfriend, they couldn't be all that serious, right?

Squeak, squeak, squeak.

Calder frowned. Even in his own head, he sounded crazy. "When will you be home? Not that this is your home, but it kind of is—well, you know what I mean." Since she'd started caring for Quinn, Calder had backed way off from his own parenting duties. Aside from changing the occasional diaper or playing with his son, he really didn't have all that much to do with the boy. Probably not a good thing, but it was what it was.

Though in his own defense, Calder had taken Quinn back to the park all on his own—twice. He'd even wrangled the kid into the safety seat. Maybe he'd go again today.

"I shouldn't be later than four. Is that all right?"

"Sure." It was already ten. How hot of a date could she have with that little time? He was more relieved than he should be that she hadn't asked for even more time off— like overnight!

"Thanks." She knelt to kiss the top of Quinn's head. "I'll miss you, sweetie."

What about me?

"WHAT DO YOU THINK she's doing?" Calder's SEAL pal Cooper dragged his chip through store-bought guacamole.

On the apartment's big-screen TV, Florida pummeled Georgia.

"Beats me." Before Quinn, Calder had also shared the apartment with Cooper, Mason and Heath. He'd been in his house a month, but he'd lived here with his friends for over three years, meaning this place felt more like home.

"If she is on a date, the guy didn't put much thought into it," Cooper said.

"That's good, right?"

His friend shot him a dirty look. "Maybe for you, but not her. This woman is caring for your kid. The key to you and Quinn being happy is keeping her happy."

"Good point." What Calder didn't understand was why Pandora's pretty smile and green eyes refused to leave his head.

He grabbed another chip and ran it through the guac. Now that he thought about it, Pandora's eyes were a unique, avocado green. He'd always liked avocados.

Quinn fussed in his carrier seat.

Calder offered him a bottle, but that didn't help. His diaper was dry and the kid pitched the pacifier Calder offered. "What do you think he wants?"

"Pick him up." Cooper shoved several chips into his mouth at once. "When my brother was a baby, lots of times he just wanted to be held."

"Makes sense." Calder squatted, scooping the infant up with one hand.

"You're not doing it right." His friend took the baby, pushing Calder out of the way. "Like this." The fact that Cooper hadn't held a baby in a couple decades, yet instantly put Calder's son at ease, incensed him. "You've got to hold him close. Let him know you care."

Do I? The thought killed Calder. He didn't want to be *that* guy—the kind of dad who never connected with his son. No way could he live with eighteen years passing only to realize he'd screwed up everything and his own kid was a virtual stranger. They'd connected at the park, so why not now?

Calder took advantage of Heath and Mason being out on a beer-and-pizza run. "Mind if I ask you a personal question?"

"Shoot."

"I'm not even sure where to start." He tilted his head back, working the muscles on his suddenly tight neck. "You guys all know how Quinn entered my life, and I guess I'm still struggling to form a connection with the little guy. I feel like I should have this instinctive draw toward him, you know? But most days, I'm not even sure what he likes to eat—let alone how to really be a good dad. My own father was hardly a prizewinning specimen, but you come from a great family, right? Since you had a great dad, I was hoping you might share a few pointers."

Cooper snorted. "Hate to be the bearer of bad news, but

you hit up the wrong guy for that information. My advice?" He returned Quinn to Calder. "Buy a parenting book."

PANDORA HUGGED her daughter for all she was worth, then gently pushed her back for a better look. "You've grown an inch since the last time I saw you."

Julia laughed. "Mom Cindy calls me her pretty sunflower 'cause I'm growing so big and tall and pretty!"

"You're beyond pretty," Pandora said past the lump in her throat. "You're gorgeous."

The social worker assigned to Julia's case sat in the corner of the pale blue room with its one window that was meant to be cheerful, but how many times had Pandora been here, praying one day she'd take her daughter home? How many other parents like her were on the same seemingly sinking ship? She'd taken state-mandated parenting courses. She'd proved herself capable of holding a job. Still, in the court's view it wasn't enough. Would it ever be enough?

"Look what I made on vacation!" Her daughter proudly displayed a leaning tower made of driftwood, pebbles, shells and gobs of glue. "Mom Cindy said it's the most *beautifulist* thing she's ever seen."

"She's right." The admission was difficult when all Pandora wanted was to scratch *Mom Cindy*'s eyes out. Jealousy may have consumed her, but she'd come too far to let it show. She'd learned a good mother puts her child's needs ahead of her own, and given how precious little time they had this afternoon, that's exactly what she'd do. "Tell me about the beach. Was it fun?"

While Julia shared tales of jumping into the waves and building a *humongous* castle with her fun new beach toys, Pandora drank it all in, wondering at the coincidence—the cruel twist of fate—of them both experiencing their first day at the shore with different people.

Hanging on to her daughter's every word, it occurred to Pandora that far from being angry with the foster parents assigned to their family's case, she should be grateful. Julia's *Mom Cindy* was a shining example of how the system was supposed to work.

"What's in there?" Julia pointed to the floral gift bag that had pink curly ribbon cascading from the top.

"Gosh, I don't know…" Pandora couldn't resist tugging her girl into another hug. "I was so interested in hearing about your adventure, I forgot what's in the bag."

"No, you didn't." Julia's giggle acted as a balm to Pandora's weary soul. "Tell me, tell me!"

"Okay…" Pandora handed her daughter her gift. "But I don't know if you'll like it."

"I will! I will!" The little girl added jumps to her giggles while tossing the ribbon from the bag. First, she took out a small Junie B. Jones doll, then three of the first books in the series outlining the turbulent, yet hilarious, tales of the girl's kindergarten experience. Largely due to Pandora's mistakes, Julia was starting first grade, though she should have been entering second grade. "She's pretty! I love her!"

"These books tell all about what happens to her at school. I thought it might be fun to sit and read them together. What do you think?"

Julia nodded. "Mom Cindy reads to me. It's nice."

"I'm glad, sweetie. Always remember, books are your friends." Seated on a too-stiff formal sofa, Pandora made the best of the awkward situation by patting the cushion alongside her. "Come over here and let's find out what happens…"

Turned out the social worker was a Junie B. fan and hadn't heard the stories since her own child had been small. The three of them laughed together until it was time for Julia to meet back up with her foster parents. Though it was harder than anything she'd ever done, Pandora thanked them for providing such a stable foundation for her daughter.

Then the visit was over.

During the long drive to Calder's, she indulged in a nice long cry. Better to get her tears out privately. Quinn deserved her best, and spending the remainder of her day weepy certainly wouldn't solve the many problems of her own making. For those, the only solution was time. At least now she'd pass that time in a comfortable environment where she knew she'd make a positive difference.

The closer she came to the house, the more her pulse raced with the realization that she was excited to see her sweet charge.

What about his criminally handsome father?

Pandora chose to ignore that thought. She also wanted to forget how she'd fought the strangest urge to give Calder a proper hug goodbye that morning.

Madness. But she supposed, given their forced proximity and the fact that they'd essentially become a ready-made family, her reaction was understandable. As long as she understood the reasons behind her feelings, she could ignore them and keep her primary goal in mind—regaining custody of Julia. Nothing else mattered.

Pandora pulled into the driveway and pressed the button on the automatic garage-door opener, her mouth dry, pulse racing as if returning to this happy place was her own special gift—one that Calder had made possible.

Once inside, anticipation filled her to see him and his son.

Only, they weren't there.

Despite the fact that Calder's car was gone, Pandora looked everywhere. Bedrooms. Living room. Backyard.

When her fruitless search led to her sitting alone on the couch, she kicked off her sandals, drew her feet up beside her then resigned herself to wait.

BY THE TIME Calder got home, he had heartburn from too many of Cooper's hot wings, the Gators had lost by ten and Quinn was squalling. All in all, it'd been a less than stellar day. Seeing Pandora's car already in the garage should've made him feel better, but it didn't.

Calder felt stupid for ever even asking her to the beach. From here on out, he vowed to play it cool. Hell, she worked for him, meaning he wasn't *playing* at all.

He always had trouble getting Quinn from his car seat and this time proved no different. By the time Calder held him safely in his arms, he was surprised the kid could breathe through his screams.

In the living room, Calder found Pandora crashed on the sofa.

She woke in a heartbeat, rushing to take the inconsolable baby. "What's wrong?" she crooned in the kind of ethereal-soft tone his son seemed to love. "Poor baby. Your diaper feels dry." To Calder, she asked above the wailing, "Is he hungry?"

"Could be." He dumped the diaper bag on the nearest chair. "Hell, I don't know. He's been crying the whole way home. It hasn't been *that* long since he had his last bottle, but you know how time can get away from you when a game's on."

She cast him an incredulous look.

Her attention back to his son, she said, "Let's get some nice formula in your tummy, then you'll feel better."

Somehow, Pandora managed to not only hold his son, but fix a bottle and hum all at the same time. Once she held the bottle to Quinn's lips, greedy suckling commenced, making Calder feel like the world's most inept father. What was wrong with him? How could he have let his infant son get this hungry?

In under a few minutes, Quinn had almost drained the bottle and his eyes had drifted closed.

Pandora relocated to the living room sofa, cradling Quinn while still humming her song.

In an angry whisper she said, "I left premade bottles for you in the fridge. Didn't you even look?"

"Sure, and I took all of them and he drank them. Maybe I gave them to him too soon, and then he was crazy hungry later? You tell me." Plenty miffed, Calder crossed his arms. "You're the expert."

She shook her head. "You're impossible."

"I'm good—*great*—at a lot of things, but infant care isn't one of them. I never signed on for this."

"Really?" She laughed, but the sound struck him as cold. "News flash—the moment you chose to sleep with Quinn's mom without protection…? You pretty much signed a life-long contract."

"Sorry I'm not perfect like you."

Calder had expected a snappy comeback—what he got was a whole lot of silence, then tears.

He followed her when she went to the nursery to change Quinn's diaper, brush his tiny teeth then tuck him into his crib. Only when she'd turned out the nursery lights and quietly shut the door did she respond. "For the record, I'm about as far from perfect as anyone can get. Good night."

He wanted to say more—a helluva lot more, but she'd ducked into her own room and shut that door, too.

"IF YOU WANT my opinion, let it go."

With Quinn happily batting at the stuffed cow hanging from his carrier's handle, Pandora paced her friend's office. "I know, but Calder hit a nerve with that one. Worse—here I was lecturing him for being a bad parent when I'm pretty sure I'm featured in the Lousy Parent Hall of Shame."

Natalie left her desk to wrap Pandora in a hug. "Trust me, there are worse parents out there than you. If I hadn't seen with my own eyes how hard you've worked to turn your life around, I wouldn't have believed it. You're a textbook example of how to make lemons into lemonade."

"But am I?" Sitting in the guest chair, Pandora slid her fingers into her hair. "Saturday, during my time with Julia, she kept bringing up her foster mom, Cindy, and I was so jealous I could've screamed."

"I presume you didn't?"

"No, but…" She wrung her hands. "What if I had? What's inside me that makes me want to snap?"

Her friend took the seat alongside her. "Could it be you're human?"

Outside, the day was gloomy. Earlier, there'd been storms, but for now a light drizzle had settled in. The air held just enough of a nip to remind her of the rapidly approaching fall.

The weather suited Pandora's mood.

After Saturday's visit with Julia, she'd been on top of the world. Returning to Calder's empty house had been mood dampening. But then when he had returned with his cranky son, her spirits had gone from bad to worse. She'd imagined them maybe sharing a nice dinner, then watching TV before putting the baby to bed. What really happened had left her on edge and unable to sleep for hours. Why had she let him get to her? Deep down, maybe she feared his belief that she was the image of perfect motherhood might lead to potential disaster when—*if*—he ever learned her truth.

"What're you thinking?" Natalie asked.

"Wish I knew." Leaning forward, Pandora rested her elbows on her knees, covering her face with her hands. "Calder's my boss—nothing more. I owe him zilch but my promise to give excellent care to his son."

"You're not falling for him, are you?"

"No." Pandora laughed. "That's ridiculous. I barely know him. Besides, things between us are strictly professional." *Except for the way my pulse races every time his gaze meets mine.*

"So what's the problem?"

She glared at her friend. "If I knew, I wouldn't be here, would I?"

Lips pressed tight, Natalie seemed to think an awfully long time before she said, "Please don't take this the wrong way, but are you afraid that if Calder finds out you lost Julia, he may fire you?"

"Honestly?" Pandora sighed. "That's exactly what's wrong. This is the best job I've ever had. Assuming I still have it by the time I get Julia back, I suppose I'll tell Calder everything, but until then…?" She gazed outside. "Guess I'd like him to get to know the current me as opposed to the wretched person I used to be."

PANDORA STAYED AT Natalie's office longer than she'd planned. By the time she returned to Calder's house, she noted his motorcycle parked in the garage. Despite still being upset with him for the way they'd left things the previous night, she hated that he'd ridden home from work in the rain.

Entering the kitchen through the back door, she held Quinn in the crook of one arm and her purse and diaper bag with her other.

Calder stood at the kitchen counter sipping from a mug filled with steaming, fragrant coffee. He wore no shirt and a pair of Go Navy sweats. His hair looked damp. His chiseled profile was so strikingly handsome, her mouth went dry and her pulse skyrocketed.

"Why didn't you call me?" was the first stupid thing she thought to say. "I could've picked you up."

"No biggie. I didn't mind getting wet. Besides, it's not as if you were here, waiting by the phone." He winked.

She set her keys and bags on the kitchen table.

Awkward silence between them took on a physical hum.

"About last night," he finally said after a gulp of his coffee. "I—"

"I owe you an apology. That crack about a condom—it was completely inappropriate and unprofessional. Won't happen again." She glanced down at her tiny charge. His grin not only warmed her through and through but made her wonder what she was doing. She knew the only reason she'd been upset with Calder had more to do with her own insecurities rather than anything he'd done. How many times had she been too drunk to pick up Julia from day care? Or too broke to buy milk—let alone cereal? "I just hated hearing Quinn cry and it set me on edge."

"Understandable. His crying had me almost crazy." He sighed. "I'm sorry for that snap about you being perfect. But you have to know, compared to me, you pretty much are." He held out his hand for her to shake. "Truce?"

"Yeah." When she pressed her palm to his, her fingers to his, her every nerve ending pulsed. The attraction she felt for him was unlike anything she'd felt before. Unnerving in the way his lightest touch made her crave more. But Julia was her only priority. Getting close to her boss wasn't even an option.

"Cool." He opened the fridge. "What's your plan for dinner?"

She looked at him, then Quinn, then laughed. "What do you want?"

"Anything that doesn't come from a bag or box. If I pay extra, could I bribe you into making more of your meat loaf—a double batch so there's enough for leftovers and sandwiches?"

"No bribe necessary. Assuming we have all the ingredients, it'd be my pleasure." Her only request was that Calder either leave the room or put a shirt on!

Chapter Six

"Get the lead out, Calder!"

"Yessir, Master Chief!" All afternoon—two weeks after his fight with Pandora—Calder's SEAL team had been practicing counterterrorism drills by entering a suspected terrorist compound and securing the perimeter in under a minute. After three hours of running a simulated rat-hole maze, they'd finally gotten times down to a minute thirteen seconds, but that wasn't good enough. In a real-life situation, those seconds could mean the difference between successfully completing a mission and being shipped home in a body bag.

Over and over Calder ran the drill with the rest of his buddies—his team. The men had become his family. He'd do anything for them and knew they'd return the favor.

The harder he worked, the more he focused on the reasons he did what he did. He had always thought he'd become a SEAL for the cool factor. There was no denying the title carried with it incalculable bragging rights. But the longer he wore his Trident, the more he realized it meant so much more.

Now not only did he want to be of service to his country but he also wanted to protect his son. Before having Quinn, the seedier portions of the world had been his warrior playground. Now he recognized the world's danger zones hid terrorists intent on not only harming his son, but every man, woman and child in America and beyond.

In short, like it or not, Quinn had given Calder a maturity he hadn't before possessed. He used the newfound drive to keep his kid smiling to dig deep, finally busting through the mental wall that had held him back all day.

"Fifty-seven seconds! Good work!" His CO patted his back.

While Heath splashed bottled water onto Calder's overheated face, Calder dropped to his knees. Damn glad the ordeal was over, but also proud. If the team could accomplish the task here at home, then overseas, with adrenaline pumping, there would be no question about them performing like a well-oiled machine.

While the last few on their team completed time tests, Heath and Calder sat against the base of a mock concreteblock Iraqi apartment building.

After gulping more water, Heath asked, "How's it going with the nanny?"

"Good and bad."

"Yeah?" Calder's friend raised his eyebrows. "How so?"

"On the one hand, the house has never been cleaner, my laundry's always done and as you've probably noticed, I'm headed out early to eat home-cooked meals every night."

"Sounds good so far."

"This is where things get dicey. I pay her for the basics, but the longer she's with me, the more I look forward to more. To just seeing her. And then there are those awkward late-night meetings when she's all mussed and forgets her glasses…" Calder shook his head and sighed. "I have to keep reminding myself she's my employee. Worse, when it comes down to it, I know nothing about her. Sure, her work references checked out, but I'm still wondering where she disappears to sometimes on Saturdays."

"Have you asked?" Heath tugged an energy bar from his right sleeve pocket, tore the wrapper and took a bite.

"Hell, no. It's none of my business."

"Then why are you whining to me about it?"

Calder snatched a pebble from the ground beside him and pitched it at his "friend."

FRIDAY MORNING, PANDORA fed Quinn and his father. Once Calder headed off to work, she tidied the kitchen and the rest of the house—a task that took a whopping fifteen minutes, considering she didn't have much to work with.

She hadn't forgotten that Calder had told her he'd paint her bedroom, but she wasn't sure how to broach the subject without sounding greedy. Most days, in presenting her with the opportunity to save a generous amount of money while at the same time living in a safe, quiet, fresh-smelling environment seemed like blessing enough. Sure, walls the shade of lemon sorbet would be lovely, but they were hardly a necessity when she'd once relocated from a highway underpass to a crack house to a jail cell.

With chores finished, she said to Quinn, "Looks like a gorgeous day. Want to go swing?"

"Rahee..." Quinn smiled and drooled.

"I'll take that as a yes."

Five minutes later, she'd worked his chubby arms into a light jacket, added a pint-size baseball cap then settled him in his stroller.

She left through the garage, netting a pleasant surprise to find the neighbors just east of the house were holding a garage sale. There were even a couple more down from there.

Some of the few happy memories she had of her early childhood were of visiting Saturday-morning sales with her mom and dad. They'd viewed the outings as fun, but also a necessary way to cheaply furnish their home. The items hadn't seemed shabby to Pandora, but well-worn and loved— the furniture equivalent of the dog pound.

During the first months of her marriage, she'd gone to lots of sales, intent on transforming their rented house into a home, but then her ex had lost his job and taken out his every frustration on her. Usually sporting a black eye, she'd been too humiliated to leave the house.

Doubling back inside Calder's home, she took her wallet from her purse and tucked it in the back pocket of Quinn's stroller.

The first sale didn't hold much of interest. Beyond a half-dozen paperbacks she selected for herself, many tables were laden with baby clothes, but strictly for girls. Pandora did snag a stack of picture books for a dollar and an electronic crib mirror for Quinn to play with. There were lots of fun shapes and when he pressed them, they made silly noises. He *boinged* all the way to the next sale.

"Good morning," said an older man, one of Calder's neighbors.

"Good morning." Pandora greeted him with a warm smile. "You sure picked a gorgeous day for a sale."

"Wasn't me but the wife. She's chairwoman of the Neighborhood Beautification Committee. All proceeds go toward sprucing up the flower bed at the development's entrance."

"Thanks. I'll keep that in mind." At first, Pandora didn't see much beyond stemware and yard tools, but then she spotted a painting that would be perfect over Calder's fireplace. In the foreground, the artist had created an angry sea, yet beyond the surf, sun radiated through tumultuous clouds and the water shone with an iridescent calm. The image spoke to her. How her recent years may have been a struggle, but in the future, by the time the storm blew over and she and Julia were immersed in golden sun, everything was going to be okay. Better.

Along with the painting, she found a lovely silk flower arrangement featuring daffodils in a Blue Willow china–patterned bowl. She envisioned it on the mantel, grouped with framed photos of Calder and Quinn she'd snapped with Calder's digital camera the last time they had played blocks on the living room carpet. All told, she'd spent ten dollars—twelve after also finding a quirky strawberry-shaped cookie jar.

She set the painting atop the stroller's sun visor, then stashed the rest of her items in the bottom netting.

To Quinn she said, "Guess we'd better head home to unload before hitting the park, or you'll end up sharing your seat, huh?"

He kicked and gurgled before once again hitting the *boing* button on his new toy.

"You bought the painting." A smiling older woman approached. "Martin and I have had it over our buffet for years, but my new decorator says it has to go."

"I should thank him or her. I love it."

"I'm glad. It's easier to part with knowing it'll be enjoyed. I'm Lila, by the way. Don't you and this cutie live three doors down?"

"We do." Pandora exchanged introductions.

"That man of yours is a sight to behold." Fanning herself, Lila added, "If only I were thirty years younger…"

Martin, the man Pandora assumed to be Lila's husband, called from where he sat on a lawn chair in the garage, "I heard that!"

Lila waved off his complaint. "How long have you and your hunk been together?"

"Oh—we're not a couple." Pandora's cheeks flamed. "I'm Quinn's nanny."

"*Oh*… Forgive me. I assumed you were a family. Have to admit to being old-fashioned about young couples *shack-*

ing up instead of marrying, but that's neither here nor there. Since he's your employer, I suppose it'd be hard not to share the same roof, huh?"

"Yes, it would." Though Pandora laughed, she couldn't help but fear Julia's family-court judge having similar suspicions, which might ultimately lead to disapproval. Her stomach knotted.

Carrying on with small talk as if she hadn't a care in the world proved difficult, but Pandora muddled through a chat about the lovely weather and maybe joining the beautification committee.

Lila's attention eventually turned to another customer, at which point Pandora decided in lieu of the park, she and Quinn were off to the hardware store for a picture hanger sturdy enough to hold the painting.

At five-thirty, Pandora took a fragrant roast from the oven and even lit a few candles alongside the photos she'd placed on the mantel. She felt good about the changes, but feared Calder either wouldn't care for her taste, or would find her presumptuous for taking the liberty of decorating his house.

At the time she'd impulsively made the purchases, longings for a true home had consumed her. Quinn deserved the real deal every bit as much as Julia. For years, Pandora imagined living in homey perfection. Was it wrong she now wanted her physical world to match her rich imagination?

Stomach roiling with silly nerves, she pureed Quinn's portions of the evening's meal. When Calder still wasn't home by six, she gave Quinn his bath, played with him for a bit, read a couple of his new picture books then put him to bed.

By the time Calder did finally come home, she'd curled onto the sofa's end, immersed in one of her new paperbacks.

"Sorry I'm late." He placed his motorcycle helmet on the entry closet's top shelf.

Had he been at a bar?

"Training ran *waaay* long." He yawned. The fact that he smelled faintly of the outdoors and briny sea told her he hadn't been partying. "What smells good?" He stepped farther into the room, noticing the changes she'd made. "Dang, that picture and the candles and stuff look fancy—like something my mom would do."

Even his indirect praise made her soul sing.

"I'm liking the painting—and whoa! Who are these handsome guys?" He picked up the simple wood frame that housed the snapshot she'd taken of him and his son. "Quinn really does look like me."

She put down her book, hovering behind him. "Is that the first time you've seen the two of you together?"

His eyes shone, but he soon blinked them dry. "Yeah. Caught me by surprise. I mean, I know in my head he's biologically mine, but somehow I hadn't made the connection that we share physical features."

"The bigger he gets, the more similarities you'll see. Little personality quirks will pop out, too. Some good, some bad. They all make you look at yourself in a whole new way."

He gave her a long stare. "You sound like you speak from experience, but you don't have kids, right?"

What did she say? The last thing she wanted was to outright lie. On the flip side, she wasn't anywhere near ready for full disclosure.

She settled for forcing a smile. "You must be starving. Why don't you grab a shower and I'll fix you a plate?"

STANDING BENEATH THE HOT water's stinging spray, it occurred to Calder that Pandora had skillfully evaded his question. Why? On the surface, everything about her read perfection. Was he being paranoid or could she truly be hiding something?

Out of the shower, he made quick work of toweling off, then stepping into boxers, sweats and a T-shirt.

He ambled into the kitchen and found the table set for one.

Pandora stood with her back to him at the sink, her arms up to her elbows in suds. If he hadn't been intent on getting an answer to why she'd evaded his question, his mind could have all too easily traveled to erotic places.

Once he sat and took his first bite, she asked, "Is everything warm enough?"

"It all tastes great. Thanks."

Was it just him or did she also sense an elephant in the room?

He set his fork to the plate. "Have a seat."

"I would, but I need to finish up here, then check on Quinn in his playpen."

Calder looked down. Where did he even start? "You misunderstood. We need to talk."

She turned off the faucet. "H-have I done something wrong?"

She'd given him the perfect segue to tell her his suspicions. That he hoped he was reading more into this than there was, but a couple times now, she'd been evasive. On her few Saturdays off, he'd gotten the impression she didn't want him knowing where she was going or even who she was seeing. Then tonight, when he'd asked her about having kids, her whole demeanor had changed. "If you're not happy with my work…" She seemed to take inordinate care with drying a saucepan.

"Did I say that?" *I can't even say why, but my gut tells me you're hiding something.* Solely for himself, because he woke thinking of her smile, he probed, "Do you have a child?"

"You've seen my references. If I've in any way caused you to doubt my ability to care for your son, then—"

"Damn it, Pandora." When he slapped his palm to the

table she not only jumped, but tears filled her eyes. He was instantly sorry, yet at the same time he'd been trained to always follow his gut. What was going on with her that he couldn't see? Whatever it was hadn't affected her ability to give his son expert care, so why couldn't he leave it alone? On a deeper level, what was it about her that had gotten under his skin, making her—at least in his mind—so much more than someone who worked in his home? "What's with you? Some things don't add up. Your first day on the job, when you didn't have a cell or a way to even purchase groceries without calling me for help. The fact that you lived in Norfolk, yet have never been to the beach. Your two mystery Saturdays. All I'm asking is for you to be straight with me. If you don't have a kid, is there something else going on with you that I'm missing?"

"No." Raising her chin, her expression lost its earlier wide-eyed fear and tears to now read steely determination. "But if you're unhappy with my performance, I'll turn in my resignation in the morning."

WHAT JUST HAPPENED?

Pandora had wanted to run, slamming her bedroom door, but she had held tight to her cool, refusing to throw away all she'd gained on a flash of temper.

In a move that took monumental effort, she calmly left Calder for the privacy of her room.

Until Calder had listed her so-called oddities, Pandora believed she'd done a good job of hiding her true identity, but then what did that mean? Though she'd been Quinn's nanny only a short while, she already felt as if she'd grown so much. Living in this nice home with her sweet charge and a true gentleman like Calder made her feel as if she'd been bathed in a pool of light and had emerged a new woman.

The fact that Calder sensed she hadn't been one hundred

percent truthful with him had her worried, but she couldn't lose focus on the fact that he wasn't her friend, but her employer.

In a perfect world, she might have told him everything. He may have even *deserved* to know everything. But selfishly—not just for herself, but for her daughter—she needed this job. Not only was the money important, but so was the consistency of her employment record. Fran, the social worker assigned to her case, reminded her all too often how important it was for her to prove a record of stability to the judge presiding over her next court hearing.

As Natalie was Pandora's true boss, and had told her she was perfectly within her rights to not discuss Julia, then no matter how difficult it was for her to essentially hide her daughter from Calder, she had to.

There was no other choice.

When a knock sounded on her bedroom door, Pandora's stomach knotted. "Yes?"

"Can I come in?"

How would he react if she said no? She lacked the courage to find out. "Sure."

He opened the door, but didn't breach the threshold. "I probably owe you an apology, but I'm not giving it until you assure me my imagination is running overtime and that your story is as uncomplicated as you presented it to be."

"No apology necessary." Seated at the foot of her bed, Pandora wasn't sure what to do with her hands. She'd been so excited for Calder to see the small but pretty transformation she'd made with the house. And he had appreciated what she'd done, so how had their night degraded to such an ugly place? "What I would like—and from your vantage point, I probably have no right to ask—is that I need you to trust me. Respect my wish to keep the part of my life that doesn't concern caring for your son private."

He rubbed his forehead with his fingers and thumbs.

"You're putting me in a horrible position. You know I'd never win Father of the Year. But I sure as hell only want the best woman for the job raising my son. At any given moment, the world could go to shit and my team could be called in to fix it. I have to know if that happens, you're someone I can trust."

How did she prove herself a good person? A worthy person? Why couldn't she come right out and tell him she had a daughter? Simple—because if she did, Calder would never allow her to keep her job. It wouldn't matter she was highly qualified and had worked years paying for what she'd done. What would matter was she'd once been a horrible person and he'd never believe her to be anything else.

How many times had people let her down? How many times had men specifically proved they were her enemy?

In no way did she believe that of Calder, but she couldn't place her entire future with Julia in the hands of a man she barely knew. A large part of her recovery process had been recognizing her tendency to be the victim, but those days were gone. She claimed full responsibility for her actions. What Pandora wouldn't do was jeopardize her daughter's future as she had her past.

"What do you want, Calder? You know my work history checked out or Natalie's agency would never have hired me."

"Do you have a child?"

She stood only to walk to the window, staring out at the dark yard. "Lord, you're like a dog after a bone. Leave it alone. Leave me alone."

His stare grew into a palpable heat, singeing her back.

But then he left, closing the door behind him. And she sank to the floor, snatching a throw pillow from the bed to cover her face, masking tears she feared may never end.

"THIS IS A nice surprise." Natalie, the head of the agency Calder had gone through to hire Pandora, met him at her office door, extending her hand for him to shake Monday morning. "How may I help you?"

"Mind if we have a seat?" Calder nodded toward the corner sofa-and-chair arrangement. It was the same place where he'd flipped through her book of glowing client recommendations.

She gestured for him to lead the way. "I hope your arrangement with Pandora is satisfactory?"

"Actually, that's why I'm here."

"Oh?" Her eyebrows rose.

"I can't put my finger on it, but something about her feels *off.* I've asked a couple direct questions concerning her past and she never answers. Yesterday, she barely spoke at all. It's my job to be paranoid and in this case, when the woman in question spends most every day alone with my son, I have a right to be concerned."

"Of course you do." She left the sofa to open the door and called out to her secretary, "Anna, could you please bring Pandora Moore's personal reference file?" A minute later, she had the pages open in front of him. "As you can see, not only does Pandora have an assortment of exemplary letters from former clients, but she's a close personal friend. I started this agency nearly twenty years ago, and I'm proud to say I've never had one of my employees fired—or even reprimanded. My people are top-notch. That said, if Pandora has in any way engaged in behavior that caused you to feel concern for your son, then—"

"Okay, whoa…" He held up his hands. "She's been a godsend. Quinn adores her and I depend on her to an embarrassing degree, but I know she's hiding something and I need to know what it is."

Natalie stood. "Unless you're prepared to file a formal complaint against her job performance, I'm sorry, but Ms. Moore's personal life is just that—personal."

Chapter Seven

"Hell's bells," Heath said after shooting off twenty rounds on his M16. "Give it a rest."

"But what if Pandora is hiding something?" Calder's team was engaged in target practice—only, rain fell in wind-driven sheets, making their automated moving bad guys a bitch to see. The fact that he was bone-deep chilled didn't make his day brighter. Part of him regretted even going to Natalie, but another part couldn't let his suspicions go.

"Ever think there's a reason she doesn't want to talk about her past that has nothing to do with whatever nefarious reason you've dreamed up, but something more painful?"

It was Calder's turn to shoot, and he fired an embarrassing thirty-eight rounds before hitting his long-range target. That wouldn't cut it in the field, and his CO let him know.

"Another thing…" Heath annihilated his target in three shots. "All this energy you're wasting trying to solve some mystery that doesn't exist could be better spent getting to know your son. From everything you've said, Quinn's a lucky kid to have Pandora in his life. For that matter, so are you. She's not some Friday-night special out to snag a SEAL, but a sweet gal just trying to do her job."

For the remainder of the miserable afternoon, Calder focused not only on his training, but also on Heath's words.

His friend was right.

After Quinn came into his life, Calder's view of women had changed. Before becoming a father, he'd indulged in an admittedly swinging-single lifestyle. He'd made it clear to whoever he was with that his objective on any given night was to achieve the ultimate good time. Now part of him wondered if Quinn's mother had intended to trap him. But was that paranoia, too? Was his real problem with Pandora the fact that she was so good with Quinn that she made him look all the worse in his role as a father?

If that was the case, he was a jackass.

Now the only question was, what could he do for Pandora to make up for his lousy behavior?

The rain stopped and he'd almost made it to his bike when his cell rang. He glanced at the call display.

Crap. His mom.

He loved her dearly, but lately, whenever she called, she lectured and nagged. Still, she was his mother, so he forced a smile, then answered. "Hey."

Twenty minutes later, Calder had been thoroughly chastised for not retiring from the navy in order to find a more stable job. He let it flow in one ear and out the other. His work was his one true love. Lots of SEALs had kids. They worked around them, just as he was learning to do. He told his mother the same.

"But Quinn is a baby," she said. "You talk about him like he's a friend's dog you regret agreeing to watch."

"You're being dramatic. Quinn and I are getting along just fine. Better, even." He told her about Pandora, skipping the portion about his misgivings.

"I look forward to meeting her. It's good Quinn finally has stable, reliable care."

"Agreed." After a few more minutes of small talk, Calder said, "Hate to cut you short, but I need to go."

"I understand. Oh—but before I forget, Harold has a late-

October conference in North Carolina. The resort is in the mountains and he asked me to tag along. How about the three of you come, too?"

"Thanks for the invite, but I'll have to get back to you."

Calder hung up not sure what to think.

A family vacation? Seemed odd, considering only two out of three of them were related. On the other hand, when it came down to it, he felt closer to Pandora than he had to any woman in a long time. A weekend outing would be perfect for Calder to not only mend fences but once and for all solve Pandora's mystery.

"You're so kind to think of us," Pandora said to Lila, who stood on the front porch shaking off her umbrella. The neighbor from whom she'd purchased the painting had brought still-warm banana bread Pandora couldn't wait to taste.

"Don't thank me just yet." The woman withdrew a soggy Neighborhood Beautification Committee pamphlet from her raincoat's oversize pocket, passing it along with the bread. "Mind if I come in?"

"I'm sorry, of course. You must be freezing." Pandora took Lila's offering, then stepped aside, holding open the door.

"Actually, I love the rain. I grew up on the Oregon coast. We moved out here when my husband, Martin, was in the navy and never moved back."

Unsure how to respond, Pandora was glad when her visitor caught sight of Quinn in his walker.

"Look at that cutie!" Lila slipped off her coat and rain boots, leaving them on the tiled entry floor, then aimed straight for the baby. "Our grandkids are in St. Louis. Martin and I have tossed around moving there to be with them, but with the housing market being what it is…" She shrugged.

"Being away from your family must be hard." Pandora

sat on the brick hearth. "You should at least try putting your house on the market. The worst that can happen is it doesn't sell, but if it does…?" She grinned. "You're back to being a full-time grandma."

"I like your thinking." Lila smoothed Quinn's hair, sitting cross-legged on the floor beside him. "Which brings me back around to the reason for my visit."

Pandora waved the pamphlet. "I'm guessing you're looking for warm bodies to pick up litter?"

Laughing, Lila asked, "Am I that transparent?"

"Just a little, but that's okay. I'd love to help."

"I knew I had a good feeling about you." When Lila leaned in close to make a silly face for Quinn, he stole her glasses.

"Sorry." Instantly on her feet, Pandora rescued the plastic frames just after they'd found a new home in the baby's drooling mouth. "Glasses are his favorite toy. Hold on a sec and I'll wash them for you."

With Quinn safely corralled in his walker, and Lila blowing raspberries for him, Pandora swiftly cleaned her guest's glasses, then returned them.

"That was fast." She gestured to Pandora's own glasses. "I'm guessing you could launch a side career of washing eyewear?"

"You'd be right."

After small talk about the still-pouring rain and how the committee's next meeting was Thursday morning for a trash-cleanup walk, Lila caught Pandora off guard. "Not to change the subject, but how are things progressing between you and Quinn's daddy? I know I said I'm old-fashioned about young folks living together, but I've seen the three of you walking to the park and you make the sweetest family."

It took every ounce of Pandora's self-restraint not to scowl. If only Lila had seen the *happy couple* last night…

THOUGH PANDORA HAD POLITELY shrugged off Lila's comment, now that four hours had passed and it was almost time for Calder to be home, she couldn't deny her pulse had picked up or the fact her mouth had gone dry—only this time, not in anticipation, but dread.

When he'd left that morning without saying a word, the tension had been unbearable. What he didn't know was that she'd already lived that sort of life with her ex and now wanted no part of it.

A key to her continued sobriety was steering clear of situations that made her crave the escape she'd once sought in booze and eventually pills. Far from resenting her arrest, she now recognized it for what it'd been—rescue from a downward spiral she wasn't sure she'd have survived.

When the familiar sound of Calder working his key in the lock finally came, Quinn was giggling to a Baby Einstein DVD and she sat on the hearth folding a basket of baby pants and T-shirts.

Tension balled in her stomach, making her afraid to even look his way.

"Hey, bud." Quinn had been lolling on his favorite blanket in front of the TV, but upon catching sight of his dad, the baby crawled to meet him. "Dang, you're getting fast."

Calder swooped Quinn up for a cuddle, then sat opposite her on the sofa. For the longest time he said nothing.

She kept folding until the tension between them felt tangible. Like rogue waves slamming a pier until it leaned and groaned and the wood cried with the effort to hold.

And then, temporary relief came when Calder finally spoke. "My dad's been married five—maybe six times. Can't keep it straight. He's been lied to and cheated on, but considering he gives as good as he gets, I can't work up too much emotion other than pity for the guy." Smoothing Quinn's hair, Calder seemed lost in thought. His introspection struck Pandora as vulnerable. Never having seen this imperfect side of him—aside from his lackluster child-care skills—she found herself admiring his honesty. "When you avoided my questions, I assumed you were hiding something. Automatically, my brain leaped to the dark side. But this morning, I went to the agency where I found you—spoke with Natalie—and pretty much had my ass handed to me on a platter."

"Oh?"

"Your friend told me you hung the moon. Meanwhile…" He shook his head. "My whole adult life, the only thing I've been loyal to is the U.S. Navy. I—"

"Calder, stop." Pandora continued folding, not feeling strong enough for a heart-to-heart. He was her employer. Period. The temptation to confide in him was great, but it was also dangerous. "I'm hardly a saint."

"Yeah, but judging by how nurturing you've been to not only Quinn, but even me, I'm pretty sure what's in your past can't trump the kind of guy I've been." He stared out the living room window. "Aside from my SEAL brotherhood, my policy has been to have fun without getting close."

"In regard to women?" Where was he going? Why had her heartbeat turned erratic?

He nodded. "Now that I have Quinn, I've been forced into commitment. As much as we both depend on you, that makes another commitment. For a guy who doesn't commit…" Shaking his head, he blasted her with a smile so potent it took her breath away, as well as her ability to think. "Hell, I'm in quicksand without hope of rescue."

"I—I understand." How many times had Pandora found herself in a similar position, only for far different reasons? What she didn't understand was why his explanation of why he regretted digging into her past made her feel guilty. And sad. His gut instincts about her were right. What kind of person did that make her to let him go on believing he was wrong?

Snap out it! her conscience demanded.

Plain and simple, her secretive actions had been dictated by circumstance. She was a woman hell-bent on regaining custody of her daughter. Opening herself to this man, no matter how amazing on the surface he may seem, was not an option.

"THANK YOU FOR doing the dishes, but I could've handled them."

"Did I say you couldn't?" Long after dinner and Quinn's bedtime rituals, Calder glanced up from the tech manual he'd been studying. Pandora and Quinn had taken an after-dinner walk in the park. She'd picked wildflowers and used a drinking glass for a vase. The arrangement now sat on the mantel. The flowers were pretty, but not nearly as attractive as Pandora.

"I didn't mean to sound like I was complaining." She sat on the hearth. "Just, well…thanks." She'd removed her glasses, resting them atop her head. She had a simplicity he found intriguing. Never any makeup or high-maintenance hair—just a natural beauty he very much appreciated.

"You're welcome." He placed the manual on the coffee table, far more interested in studying the ten shades of green in her eyes. "Considering all you do for me and Quinn, I wanted to return the favor."

Her smile warmed him through and through. Made him wonder why he'd ever doubted her being anything other than wholesome perfection. But then, even if he weren't her boss, it wasn't as if he had anything to offer. She deserved better than a guy genetically incapable of commitment—even if in Quinn's case he'd been thrust into it.

"Whatever the reason, I appreciate it."

"Sure." Her sweet, simple smile left him tongue-tied. He usually knew just what to do and say around women, but around her he couldn't even think. He met her gaze, which only made him more confused. Lord, he wanted to kiss her. Not the kind of boozy, dance-floor-make-out kiss he'd grown accustomed to, but more of a leisurely getting to know her in a way wholly inappropriate for a boss to know his employee.

Looking away for his own sanity, he found the perfect answer to his conversational dilemma in the sliver of her god-awful bedroom wall visible from his vantage. "Got anything going on this weekend?"

She shook her head.

"Want to paint your room?"

Nodding, voice barely audible, she said, "Sounds fun." Her words were encouraging. Her expression read wistful. Lost. Was it possible she'd craved that kiss as much as him?

SATURDAY MORNING AT Lowe's, staring at hundreds of yellow paint samples, Pandora could hardly contain her excitement. Her heart felt composed of confetti and glitter. The only thing that would make the moment even better was the day she chose wall colors for her own home she'd share with Julia.

"What do you think?" she asked Quinn, who was too busy chewing a teething hippo to do anything other than drool.

"Rah baa haa!"

"He's not a lot of help." Calder had been at the other end of the aisle selecting rollers and paintbrushes.

"That's okay." As many nights as she'd lain awake at the halfway house, dreaming of the day she'd finally live in a place to call home, she'd committed her lemon-sorbet shade to memory. The house she shared with Calder may only technically be her home because she worked there, but for now that was good enough. "I know exactly the color I want."

"Since you spend so much time in the kitchen, want it yellow, too?"

"If it's not too much trouble, that'd be nice."

He waved off her concern, then performed a smile-and-wink combo that turned her legs to mush. The man really was criminally handsome. When he turned on his charm, she craved the kind of physical attention a woman shouldn't want from her boss. She had to remember Julia came first. "You forget who you're dealing with. I've been trained to handle *any* situation with ease."

Famous last words.

Four hours into their project, Calder had more paint on him than the walls. "What am I doing wrong?"

She laughed. "Not that I'm an expert, but you're tackling the job like—" she took a second to think "—I don't know, like you're charging up some hill with a bayonet instead of a paint roller."

"A bayonet, huh?"

There he went again with his slow, easy grin. Her pulse skipped as if she was a little girl holding a carnival balloon. "Here…" She cupped her hand around his wrist, not caring that in the process, her palm got coated in paint. "Like this."

By showing him the seemingly simple movement, her whole world turned upside down. Somehow he now stood behind her, pressed against her in an innocent yet perilous way. The easy up-and-down motion of the roller called to mind other activities men and women do to a similar rhythm and suddenly the heat, the longing was more than she could bear.

She tried turning away, but only made a bigger mess of things by facing him, gazing up at lips she wasn't allowed to wonder about kissing.

"Am I doing it right?"

"Uh-huh…." How was she supposed to answer when he wasn't doing anything at all other than standing there, radiating heat and a foreign erotic hum that rendered her dizzy-drunk as she stared into his blue eyes?

From over the baby monitor, Quinn cried.

"I—I should check on him." Relief wobbled her legs. She had never been happier for Quinn to need her.

"Yeah." Calder stood close enough that his warm exhales landed near her nose. He smelled so good.

For a split second, she closed her eyes, imagining his sweet taste. And then she dragged herself back to reality.

The old Pandora would've ignored Quinn in favor of a frenzied roll in the hay. New-and-improved Pandora forced a deep breath, then, as gracefully as possible when her limbs were oh-so-pleasantly entangled with a hulking navy SEAL and a paintbrush and roller, extricated herself from the situation.

"Duty calls." She ducked under Calder's arm to escape to the hall bathroom where she washed paint from her hands. A glance in the mirror showed dilated pupils and flushed skin. The lovely shade of lemon sorbet marked her breasts where they'd brushed against Calder's chest.

Cheeks superheated, nipples mortifyingly hard, she craved a drink almost as badly as Calder's touch.

The thought scared her.

Brought her down from the clouds to scurry into Quinn's room where she addressed the infant's needs instead of her own.

Chapter Eight

Pushing midnight, with Quinn long asleep, bone-deep exhaustion settled over Calder—only not from the physical exertion of painting, but from keeping his hands off his son's nanny.

Calder sat on one side of the kitchen floor, leaning against the cabinets. He sat on the floor because Pandora said he was too dirty to sit on the furniture and she was right.

She sat opposite him, daintily plucking green peppers from her pizza and setting them in a soggy pile on the edge of her plate.

"When I ordered," he asked, "why didn't you tell me of your apparent green-pepper aversion?"

"If you like them, it's not a big deal for me to take them off." Having finally completed her task, she took her first bite and smiled. "Mmm. I didn't realize how hungry I was."

She smiled again as she chewed. A good three hours earlier, her ponytail had gone crooked, and yellow now streaked her cheeks and hair. Yellow overspray from the roller speckled the lenses of her glasses. He had never seen her looking more lovely. And he had never wanted a woman more, yet been so keenly aware he couldn't have her. Was that the force driving his attraction? The fact that she was off-limits?

"Green peppers aside," Calder asked after his second slice, "when's the last time you did something nice for yourself?"

"All the time." She sipped her cola. He'd offered her a beer, but she'd declined.

"Like what?"

"Last Friday, Quinn and I went to some yard sales again. We had a great time."

"Yeah, but all you bought were things for my house or Quinn."

"I grabbed a few books for myself. And those two throw pillows. And I forgot to mention it, but I met one of the neighbors and even joined her club. Quinn and I are now official members of the Neighborhood Beautification Committee."

"That sounds indulgent," he teased after finishing his brew.

She rolled her eyes. "You sound like one of those morning talk shows where they have some expert talk about how stressed we all are, and how women should indulge themselves by soaking in bubble baths or frolicking in potpourri."

I'd like to see you frolic—naked.

That thought sent Calder reaching for another beer.

"For me anyway, all that's a crock. I wasted a lot of time doing only what I wanted in life and it cost me—dearly." She shrugged, "May sound cheesy, but now I get more satisfaction from making other people happy."

"Makes sense." Whoa. Had the mysterious Pandora Moore actually opened up? He almost asked what specifically she'd lost, but then thought better. Interrogation wasn't his strongest suit, but he knew enough to recognize he'd learn more from carefully listening to her than pressing for answers. Besides, she was a genuinely nice person. Aside from his team members, he hadn't met all that many.

"Thank you for my lemon sorbet." She was back to plucking green peppers. "Once we clean all the drips and put everything back in place, your house will be very pretty."

It was on the tip of Calder's tongue to tell her no house

could be as pretty as her, but even though the statement would've been true, she deserved more than his old brand of clichéd *cheese*. "I think so, too. Might also make it more homey for Quinn."

She nodded, then rose to put her plate in the dishwasher. She held out her hand for his.

"Thanks."

"No problem." She stared at him a moment too long. "You must be exhausted."

"Trust me, I've had worse days." He joined her in clearing the small dinner mess and putting away what remained of their meal. "Tell me about this club you and Quinn joined."

"It's no big deal." She leaned against the counter and shrugged. "Just a friendly group helping to keep the park and main entrance areas clean. I really like the woman who leads it. Her name's Lila. She's a grandmotherly type. Quinn took an instant liking to her, too."

"Nice." He wiped down the counter. "He doesn't get to see much of my mom—which reminds me, we're invited for a long weekend with her and my stepdad at some resort. Interested?"

"When?" Just like that, her mood turned evasive again. She'd darted her gaze and drew in her lower lip.

"Third weekend in October."

She took a moment to ponder this, then smiled. "Sure."

The issue should've been no big deal. So why was he back to wondering what she was trying to hide?

AFTER CALDER HAD gone to bed and she'd checked on Quinn, Pandora found it impossible to sleep. Her room smelled strongly of paint, but she liked the newness. The scent was faint in Quinn's room, but she'd cracked his window just in case.

While pacing her room, she could've told herself she

couldn't sleep because of excitement over their upcoming trip, and it would be true. After all, she'd never been on a true vacation—not that this was, since she'd technically be working, but just staying at the resort would be a new thrill.

She could also claim insomnia over the sheer wonder of her beautiful new room. She couldn't wait to hit more yard sales and thrift stores, finding just the right pictures and knickknacks. She'd decorate it as if it were her own. Sort of a practice run for when she and Julia finally had their own home.

The truth behind her inability to close her eyes, though, was a bit more complicated, centered around a certain SEAL whose mere presence raced her pulse.

Never having been big on small talk, she'd expected their day spent together to be agony, yet he was surprisingly easy to talk to. But maybe that was because he'd done most of the talking. He never ran out of stories and she'd very much enjoyed hearing of his many travels.

So why, then, had she opened her big fat mouth during dinner? *I wasted a lot of time doing only what I wanted and it cost me—dearly.*

Pandora covered her face with her hands.

Had Calder read anything into her statement? Surely not, or he wouldn't have invited her to meet his mother and stepdad. She was acting paranoid, but spending time behind bars did that to a person.

THE NEXT MORNING, Calder watched on while Pandora fed Quinn Cheerios and pinchable-size banana chunks and blueberries. The baby had milk in his sippy cup, but still managed to make quite a mess. He'd learned berries can be smooshed before eating. Each time he *popped* one on his high-chair tray, he giggled.

Realizing his kid had learned something—no matter how

minute—did funny things to Calder's heart. Not the touchy-feely sort, he couldn't tell whether he felt parental pride or the same garden-variety affection he would for any cute kid with purple cheeks. But then, that was also significant, because when was the last time he'd even noticed a kid other than his own?

Then there was Pandora. Hair still damp from the shower and her T-shirt clinging to certain curvy areas, he couldn't help but wonder if this little domestic scene was the real deal. If he leaned to his right, cupping her left breast, would he earn a swat and a dirty look or the sort of grown-up giggle that led to a steamy kiss?

He exhaled sharply.

This kind of thinking wouldn't do.

He shouldn't be consumed by lustful thoughts about his son's nanny. No doubt a night started at Tipsea's and ended with a hottie at the motel across the street would heal his horny afflictions.

Only trouble was he didn't want to go to a bar. He wanted to stay home with Quinn and Pandora. Which made no sense.

"What are your plans for today?" Pandora asked.

"Guess since poor Quinn got stuck watching us paint yesterday, we could do something together today? I mean, if you're available?"

"Yesterday at Lowe's, I noticed the pansies were out. If you feel up to it, we could plant a few dozen in the front flower bed. Quinn loves the park sandbox, so I'm sure he'd get a kick out of gardening."

"Not a half-bad idea. Mom always used to have me help out in the yard. Though it's been years since I've done anything but mow."

Two hours later, supplies were purchased and unloaded.

Only trouble was, when Calder looked to Pandora for guidance as to how they should proceed, she sat on the pile of three topsoil bags with Quinn on her lap, both of them looking at him.

"What next?" he asked.

She frowned. "Sorry. I've never really done anything like this. Always wanted to, but…" She lifted the hood on Quinn's sweatshirt. Clouds had moved in, turning the September day chilly.

"This whole flower plan was your idea."

Along with an adorable grin, she said, "It can't be that hard."

Calder shook his head then whipped out his phone. "I'll look it up." A minute later, he said, "I officially feel like an idiot and you should, too." He smiled to let her know he was teasing. "Pretty simple. We pluck all the weeds and existing dead crap. Dump on the new dirt. Stick the plants in the ground. If we still have energy, we can go back to Lowe's for the mulch the sales guy kept pushing."

"You're right—" another grin shot his way "—I do feel stupid." To Quinn, she asked, "Ready to get to work?"

The baby gurgled.

She sat him on the brick garden path where he proceeded to grab for anything green and shove it in his mouth. "Maybe including Quinn in this project wasn't such a hot idea."

"How about for the weeding part," Calder said, "you two supervise?"

When the old-and-married crowd at work occasionally complained about the household chores their wives had them do, Calder had always been sympathetic. He'd assumed he'd never want to be saddled with that kind of boredom. But it turned out the more he worked, the better the yard looked. His yard. *Their* yard. And for whatever reason, he liked the sound of that. Not cool for a guy who knew he could never handle true commitment.

Finished weeding, he and Quinn broke up the ground a

little with the spade they'd purchased. "There you go, buddy," he urged his son. "Stab it. Get it all nice and loose."

Quinn shrieked every time he slammed the spade into the dirt.

"Aw, he makes me wistful for when my kids were young." A woman about his mother's age approached across the driveway.

"Lila, hi." Pandora rose, giving the woman a hug. "This is Quinn's dad, Calder."

"Nice to finally meet you." She extended her hand for him to shake, but as he was as dirty as his son, they both laughed and air shook.

"Lila's the leader of the cleanup club I told you about."

"Seems like a clean-enough neighborhood." Calder sat back on his heels. "Is there enough litter that you need a whole group?"

Quinn grabbed a clump of dirt, bringing it to his mouth.

"Hold up, bud." Calder grabbed his son around the waist, swooping him onto his lap. He turned to Pandora. "Think he's hungry?"

"For finding trouble," she teased, taking the infant from him, brushing off the soil he'd gotten on his jeans and T-shirt.

"Sorry," Calder said to Lila. "Seems like ever since Quinn landed in my life, I'm always a step behind whatever mayhem he's causing."

"Comes with the territory." Lila warmly smiled. "And to answer your question, you'd be surprised how inconsiderate people can be when it comes to improper trash disposal. But trash isn't our only focus. We also beautify the entries, decorating them for holidays and such."

"That's nice." Not being all that big a fan of holidays, Calder wasn't sure what else to say. He'd spent last Christmas in Afghanistan. It hadn't been a good time.

"It means a lot to some of our older neighbors whose families are grown and far away. Reminds them of happier times."

"Sure."

"Hard to believe the three of you aren't a family." Lila fixed her smile on Quinn, tweaking his sneaker. "You seem so comfortable together."

"Yeah, well—" Calder thumbed toward his still-to-be-finished job, then the sky "—I should finish. Looks like rain."

"Of course." Lila gave Pandora another hug, asking her to stop by for coffee soon.

Once she'd left, Pandora said, "Sorry about that. I didn't mean to involve you in my club."

"Not a problem." Despite Quinn's *help,* he'd spread the fresh soil and now planted yellow flowers. "She seems nice."

"She is. But I know most men don't like to be bothered with these kinds of things."

Once again, alarm bells rang. Not wanting to alert her to the fact he found her statement—her overall behavior—odd, he kept planting. She'd reacted in a similar manner that day he'd met her at the grocery store. As if she'd grown accustomed to appeasing a hothead. Had she once been in an abusive relationship? The thought of a man doing her physical harm made him nauseous. "In case it escaped your notice, I'm not *most* men. I'm guessing it gets lonely for you, here alone all day with Quinn. I'm glad you met a friend."

"Really?"

"Yeah. Really." He glanced her way, pretending not to notice her shimmering green eyes. It took more willpower than he'd known he possessed not to flat out ask her about her past. Instead, he realized no matter what Natalie told him, for his own morbid curiosity, he had to know what Pandora had been through.

ON WEDNESDAY, PANDORA tidied the house in preparation for one of Natalie's regular home inspections. Though Pandora had nothing to be nervous about, she took extra care with scrubbing the backsplash grout behind the kitchen sink.

"Quinn," she said, "do you think all this cleaning will help your daddy want to keep me around for a nice long time?"

The boy cooed from his walker.

"Yes? Awesome!" She knelt alongside him to kiss his chubby cheek.

By the time her friend arrived, the home fairly sparkled and the air smelled rich from fresh-baked lemon poppy-seed bread.

"Wow," Natalie said as she admired the kitchen. "I love this color. Your idea or Calder's?"

Glowing from her friend's praise, Pandora busied her flighty hands by slicing them each a piece of the bread. "Surprisingly, Calder's idea to paint, but he let me pick the color, which I thought was awfully nice. Since the windows are a standard size, I've got my eye out for curtains. Although I've always thought it might be fun to learn to sew. Wonder if the thrift store ever gets sewing machines?"

"Uh-oh…" Natalie drew a chair out from the kitchen table.

"What's wrong?" Pandora redirected Quinn, who had whined when he'd gotten himself stuck in a corner.

"You're sounding awfully domestic. I've been at this job for a long time, and I'm pretty sure this is the cleanest house I've ever seen." She nibbled her bread.

"And? What's your point?" With Quinn once again happily touring the kitchen, Pandora joined her at the table.

"I don't want to see you hurt. I'm afraid you're falling for Calder and his son. This is a job—not your life. You have Julia to consider."

Natalie's words hit Pandora like a slap. "That's a horrible thing to say. More than anyone, I know my place in this house. And I sure as—" she stopped short of cursing "—I know my first and *only* priority is my daughter."

"I didn't mean to sound cruel." When Natalie covered her hand, Pandora jerked away.

"You might not have meant to, but you did." Moving away from the table, Pandora needed to hold Quinn—to remind herself he was the reason she worked so hard to make this house a home.

Really? Then why had Calder's approval come to mean so much? Why did something as simple as his enjoyment of her meat loaf fill her with a quiet contentment she'd never known?

"I'm sorry." Though her friend's tone was sincere, Pandora couldn't get past her hurt feelings—only not because of what Natalie had said, but because she knew her friend was right but didn't want to admit it. Though Julia was her top priority, she could no longer deny Quinn and his dad had taken a close second.

"It's okay." Rejoining Natalie, she rested her elbows on the table, covering her face with her hands. "Sometimes it's scary how well you know me. I do like Calder—a lot. But I swear to you nothing inappropriate has happened."

"I didn't think for a minute it had, but you know what the funny thing is?" She smiled. "I almost wish it would. Calder's a good guy. He seems shaky about the whole instant-fatherhood situation he finds himself in, but who wouldn't?"

"Bite your tongue. You're right, though. I guess I have been trying to make this place cozier than I should, but Nat, considering where I've been, is that so wrong? Jail was…" Refusing to cry, she shook her head. "Jail was a nightmare. The halfway house not much better. Every day here is a dream. Calder is…" How did she begin describing the un-expected role he now played in her life? "Well, Calder's fast becoming my friend. Aside from you, I haven't had many."

"That makes me sad."

"Up until now, I haven't deserved any." But in the almost two months she'd cared for Quinn, she felt transformed. Granted, her current role had come about through plenty of hard work, but she had done it. And now her life was better for it. "But that's changing. I've had a few good talks with a nice neighbor, and in a couple weeks I'll meet Calder's mom and stepdad."

Natalie helped herself to more bread. "They coming for a visit?"

"We're meeting them at a North Carolina resort."

"As in the three of you are going on vacation?"

Pandora couldn't help but smile. "I guess you could call it that—only I'll still be working."

"Of course." Natalie's exaggerated nod only made her smile more suspect.

Eyebrows raised, Pandora asked, "You think I won't?"

"Oh—I have no doubt you'll continue doing a great job with Quinn, but I'm more intrigued by all that alone time you'll have with his dad."

Pandora frowned. "You do realize that as my boss, you're not supposed to encourage the fraternization you keep hinting you'd like to see?"

"Sadly, yes. Which is why I'll now have to walk off the half loaf of your sinfully yummy bread I've eaten to cover my guilt."

Guilt? Natalie had no clue of the true meaning.

Pandora feared the upcoming trip would test her mightily in regard to keeping her relationship with Calder strictly professional.

More and more, the man and his adorable son felt like her new drugs. For a former addict—not a good thing.

Chapter Nine

Monday afternoon, Calder got word his team would ship out that night for Somalia. *Yay.* He had a couple hours off until returning to base, and in the past, before he'd known about Quinn, he'd be psyched about any new op. But his current feelings were more in the realm of resigned. Hopefully it'd be an in-and-out mission. Surgically clean.

It sounded selfish, but he especially wanted to be home before the North Carolina trip.

The more time he spent with Pandora, the more curious he grew. Working together in the yard, he'd sensed she may have been on the verge of opening up. He'd hoped to see even more progress tonight. Which made no sense. He had nothing to offer her in the way of any serious relationship, so why attempt making more out of their working friendship than there was?

"Hi, there!" The smile Pandora greeted him with as he climbed off his bike and removed his helmet turned his supposedly tough SEAL shell to mush. The day was warm and sunny with barely a breath of wind. She stood barefoot on the front lawn, holding Quinn's raised hands while he staggered about, perfecting his walk. "Look, Quinn! Daddy's home!"

His son's giggle raised a knot in Calder's throat.

When Pandora *walked* the baby to him, Calder lifted his

son for a hug. He would miss Quinn, as well as the boy's nanny, when he left for his mission.

Sighing, he asked, "Remember when I told you I sometimes need to ship out with short notice?"

She nodded, and damn if her eyes didn't suddenly shine with unshed tears. "But you'll be home soon, right?"

"Sure." *Home.* Such a loaded word. He used to return from missions to the apartment he shared with fellow team members. It was vacant while they were gone. An empty vessel standing by to once again be filled. Now that he had a home, a son, a woman—a *friend*—who cared for both, he feared the game may have changed.

"Okay, then…" She took a deep breath and forced a smile. "I imagine you need help packing? I just did laundry, so—"

"Thanks, but I'm good. It's not really a traditional packing kind of trip, and my gear's back on base, ready to go." He smoothed Quinn's downy hair. "I just wanted to see this guy." *You.* "Let you know I'm leaving. Make sure you have enough money and stuff."

"There's plenty in the house account."

"Good. I'll add more. And you and Quinn go have fun once in a while, okay?"

"Sure…."

There was more he wanted to say, but he wasn't sure how. Or even if it was appropriate. He wanted to thank her for all she'd done for him and Quinn. For all she would do in bringing him peace of mind while he was gone. "Look…" He glanced down. Kicked a pebble near his foot. "There's no easy way to say this, so I might as well come right out with it. If something happens and I don't—"

"Stop." She held up her hands. "You're going to be fine."

"Yeah, but if I'm not…"

She childishly put her hands over her ears and shook her head. Calder set Quinn on the grass, then clasped Pandora's wrists, gently tugging her arms down before taking her hands. Easing his fingers between hers felt as forbidden and raw as if he'd slid inside her. In all the missions he'd been on, he'd never experienced such crushing urgency to take care of business that might be left behind. Before Quinn, before Pandora, he'd always called his folks prior to leaving for a mission, then been on his merry way. Now? He gave her hands an urgent squeeze, wanting desperately to kiss her but squashing the urge. For all he knew, she viewed him strictly as her boss—as she should.

"Okay, so look," he began again. "If anything happens to me, my mom has all the necessary documentation to make sure Quinn's legally safe. Her number's in the address book I keep in the drawer under the kitchen phone."

She swallowed hard and nodded.

"I hope to be back before our North Carolina trip. I want you to meet my mom. I think you two will be friends."

"I—I'd like that."

During their exchange, Quinn had nearly crawled his way to the sidewalk. When Pandora released Calder's hands to chase after her charge, for a moment he felt bereft. He knew it was the whole going-off-to-war thing that had him melodramatic, but he couldn't help it. Was this how his pals Garrett and Deacon felt every time they left their families? If so, how did they take it? He and Pandora weren't anything but employer and employee, so why did he feel as if he was leaving not only his son, but a woman who could one day teach him that commitment might not be all bad?

"THANK YOU," Pandora said to Lila, who'd just brought her fourth batch of cookies in two weeks. She opened the front door, inviting her friend inside. "Quinn and I always appreciate your baking, but you do know you don't have to keep bringing us goodies."

"Of course, I know." She made a beeline for Quinn, who

sat on the carpet playing with his jumbo blocks. "But as long as Calder's off fighting for our country, the least I can do is bake for his family."

"I'm not his family," Pandora said for what felt like the hundredth time.

"Maybe not technically, but haven't you ever heard that old saying about there being families we're born into and then there are the ones we choose?"

"Well, sure, but..." Her words trailed off because she realized what Lila said was true. Of course, Julia was still her world, but since taking this job, her world had expanded and blossomed. Quinn meant so much to her, and no matter how vehemently she tried denying feeling anything special for his father, every night when she said her prayers, adding extra for Calder and his team's protection, her thoughts drifted to memories of that sunny morning he'd held her hands.

Had his action been significant? Or was she reading too much into what had in reality been a casual gesture? Having never been around men who weren't either physically or emotionally abusive—sometimes both—she had no experiences with which to gauge what was real.

All she did know was standing in the yard, warm sun kissing her face, she'd wished Calder had kissed her, too.

By the time Pandora's next visit with Julia rolled around, Calder was still out of town. She could've asked Natalie to watch Quinn for her, but Pandora figured her daughter would get a kick out of playing with a "real live" doll, so she packed Quinn up and took him with her.

"He's so cute," her daughter said. Julia sat in the corner of the visitation room's sofa, holding Quinn on her lap. "I love his chubby belly."

"Me, too."

"Mom Cindy's having a baby!"

"Really?" Pandora's stomach tightened into a knot. Though it wasn't something she liked thinking about, she did worry what would happen should Julia prefer Mom Cindy to her. "That's exciting." And it was. She didn't begrudge anyone else's happiness but was more than ready to claim a slice of her own.

"When I live with you again, do we get to keep Quinn?"

"No, sweetie." Worry vanished, making way for anticipation of the day she finally took Julia home. The fact that her daughter also thought of that time swelled her heart with joy, reminding her to once and for all stop fearing every little thing. "We can't keep Quinn, but as long as I work for his dad, we get to play with him all we want."

"That's good."

"I think so." She toyed with one of Julia's blond curls. Her hair was getting so long and pretty. During her few sober nights, she'd loved brushing it, singing lullabies, dreaming of a better life for them both. "Have you decided what you want to be for Halloween?"

"A princess or a zombie!"

"Oooh." Pandora made a face. "Wouldn't a zombie be too scary?"

"Probably. But Brent in my class says any costume that isn't scary is stupid. Do you think so, too?"

Peer pressure this early? "I think it's important for you to pick a costume you feel super comfortable and happy wearing. If every time you look in the mirror, you get scared, then that doesn't sound very fun, right?"

Julia giggled. "Mom?"

"Yes?" Hearing her daughter call her that was heaven on earth.

"Can you please read more of the book we started last visit?"

"I'd love to." Snuggling closer to both children, Pandora took the book from her bag, then turned the page to where they'd last left off.

ANOTHER WEEK PASSED with Calder gone.

Pandora kept busy taking Quinn for walks and teaching herself to sew using the ancient Singer she'd found for ten bucks at a yard sale. So far, she'd made kitchen curtains and a small, colorful quilt for Quinn. One day, she'd like to create clothes for Julia, but she'd need way more practice first.

Lila and Natalie often stopped by, and though Pandora's nights were sometimes lonely and long, she worked hard to maintain Quinn's schedule and to not dwell on the fact that his father was likely in constant danger.

On a Wednesday night, when she was dicing carrots to boil for Quinn's supper, the phone rang.

It didn't ring all that often, so the noise startled her and Quinn, who burst into tears.

"Poor baby, it's okay." Before answering, she plucked him off the kitchen floor and into her arms. "Hello?"

"Hi, Pandora?"

"Yes?" The woman on the line sounded familiar, but Pandora couldn't immediately place her.

"This is Patricia—we met during the guys' beach-volleyball game?"

"Oh, sure. How are you?"

"Actually, great. Now that Heath and I are officially engaged, I'm on the *wife*-calling circle. I know you and Calder aren't like a couple or anything, but I thought you'd want to know the guys are due back tomorrow afternoon."

"That's great!" Pandora didn't even try hiding her excitement, and her relief. "Thank you so much for calling."

Patricia laughed. "You're welcome. Enjoy the rest of your night."

Pandora hung up the phone and closed her stinging eyes.

"Hear that, sweetie?" She tickled Quinn's tummy. "Your daddy's coming home."

CALDER DIDN'T THINK his commanding officer would ever end their team's debriefing. Finally, it was over, and he was free to go. A long time ago, he would have hit Tipsea's for a wild night out with his single friends, but instead he shared in a few minutes' obligatory handshaking and backslapping on a job well done, then hitched a ride home from Heath.

Heath dropped him at the curb, saying a quick goodbye as he was eager for his reunion with Patricia.

With his ditty bag slung over his shoulder, Calder crossed the yard and mounted his porch steps at a hurried pace. Lord, he couldn't wait to hold his son.

And Pandora?

How did he feel about seeing her?

He didn't have to wait long to find out. She must've gotten the heads-up on his imminent arrival because she dashed out the door with Quinn in her arms. "Hi! We missed you!"

Laughing, tossing his bag to reach for his son, he said, "Not half as much as I missed you. And this guy looks like he's grown a foot."

"How was it?"

He made a face.

"Sorry." She tucked her hair behind her ears. Had it grown longer? He liked it. "Dumb question."

"Nah, I wouldn't say that past missions have been *enjoyable,* and even though this one was relatively short, it felt longer than the fifteen months I spent in Iraq."

"That's a really long time."

"No kidding." The phrase struck him as trite. There was so much Calder wanted to say but wasn't sure how, or if he should. He'd seen kids Quinn's age living in deplorable conditions. Women performing countless hours of hard physical labor to scrape a meager existence from ravaged land. When he'd been on missions before, he'd focused on getting his job done. This time, he'd soaked in the world around him, really took a good long look at the people and what they were even fighting for. It'd been sobering. And more than anything, he wanted to draw Pandora in for a hug, burying his face in her hair.

"Patricia told me you'd be home today, so if you're hungry, I made all your favorites." She gestured toward the door, smiling shyly in a way that twisted him all up inside. He'd be lying if he said he hadn't spent every second of downtime thinking about her and Quinn.

"You didn't have to do that." *But I'm sure glad you did.*

"I know. I wanted to." Tugging him by his sleeve, she urged him inside. "Come on. Quinn and I did some decorating."

Calder trailed after her, trying not to focus on her swaying hips. Looking up, he got a shock to find his living room transformed into the sort of patriotic homecoming usually reserved for the airport welcoming of National Guard units. SEALs operated without a lot of fanfare. So this...

He teared up. "Quinn," he said, locking his gaze with Pandora, "did you do all this?"

"He sure did." Pandora winked. "Although he had to sit on a few phone books to see over the wheel when he was out buying supplies."

"This is..." There were no words to describe how her simple gesture of red, white and blue balloons and streamers, coupled with a giant banner reading Welcome Home, Daddy! made him feel special. As if he'd somehow become part of a family without even knowing it. "This is really great."

When Calder's throat knotted again, he did what he'd been craving from the moment he'd set eyes on her, and gave Pandora a hug. With Quinn squirming between them, there was nothing sexy about the gesture, but it felt great all the same.

"I'm glad you like it." When she stepped back, her eyes shone. "Quinn and I had fun. He made all the handprints decorating the edge of your banner."

Holding Quinn out to face him, Calder took in his son's handiwork, then said, "I'm impressed. Looks like we've got quite the little artist on our hands." *We.* The moment he referred to both himself and Pandora, Calder knew all the time he'd spent thinking about her when he'd been in Somalia was for a reason. He had started to think of Pandora as an integral part of not only Quinn's life but his.

Whether he felt up for commitment or not, something was happening that felt out of his control. For the first time in his life, he cared for a woman. The notion was both exhilarating and terrifying.

After sharing a delicious early dinner, helping with the dishes, taking Quinn for a walk in the park then giving him his bath and tucking him in, Calder couldn't remember having ever felt more at peace.

"Help me with something," he said to Pandora when they'd both settled in the living room before a crackling fire.

"Anything." Her smile warmed him through and through.

"This is going to sound crazy, but hear me out." He leaned forward where he sat on the sofa, resting his elbows on his knees. "When we met, I operated under the assumption that you were Quinn's nanny and that was it. I never wanted anything more from life than to win a few battles for the good guys, then party every Friday and Saturday night, but now? I don't know…." He ran his fingers through his hair. "Feel free to file a lawsuit if this is off base, but…" He looked up to find her staring.

"Yes?" Hands tightly clasped on her lap, she swallowed hard.

"I like you, Pandora."

After licking her lips, she said, "I like you, too. But I can't. I mean, I shouldn't. It wouldn't be right."

"Would I be out of line asking why?"

Her lips curved into what he could only describe as a haunted smile. As if she'd been in this spot before and wasn't sure she wanted to proceed.

Only for him, this was a first. He didn't commit. He acted as irresponsibly as safety allowed, then went on his way. He wasn't proud of that fact, but that's what it was—fact. Now he found himself in the uncharted territory of not knowing where he stood, and he didn't like it.

"Sorry," he blurted, pushing to his feet. "I shouldn't have said that."

She stood, too. And then went to him, shyly easing her arms around his waist, pressing her cheek to his chest. Could she feel, hear, his heart pounding? "I *really* like you, too."

He exhaled sharply, holding her close.

"But there are things about me—my past—you need to know."

Part of him wanted to know everything about her. His more rational side told him to back away. He'd never had a girlfriend and he sure as hell wasn't interested in marriage. Which meant what?

Hands on her upper arms, he pushed her back, just far enough to finally kiss her. He'd almost touched his lips to hers, then suddenly released her to turn away. "Sorry. You're right. I can't do this, either."

FREE Merchandise is 'in the Cards' for you!

Dear Reader,

We're giving away FREE MERCHANDISE!

Seriously, we'd like to reward you for reading this novel by giving you **FREE MERCHANDISE** worth over **$20**. And no purchase is necessary!

You see the Jack of Hearts sticker above? Paste that sticker in the box on the Free Merchandise Voucher inside. Return the Voucher promptly...and we'll send you valuable Free Merchandise!

Thanks again for reading one of our novels—and enjoy your Free Merchandise with our compliments!

Pam Powers

Pam Powers

P.S. Look inside to see what Free Merchandise is **"in the cards"** for you!

HAR-FM-09/13

YOUR FREE MERCHANDISE INCLUDES...

2 FREE Harlequin® American Romance® Books

AND 2 FREE Mystery Gifts

FREE MERCHANDISE VOUCHER

2 FREE BOOKS and 2 FREE GIFTS

Please send my Free Merchandise, consisting of
2 Free Books and **2 Free Mystery Gifts**.
I understand that I am under no obligation to buy
anything, as explained on the back of this card.

154/354 HDL F43Z

Please Print

FIRST NAME

LAST NAME

ADDRESS

APT.#   CITY

STATE/PROV.   ZIP/POSTAL CODE

Offer limited to one per household and not applicable to series that subscriber is currently receiving.
Your Privacy—The Harlequin® Reader Service is committed to protecting your privacy. Our Privacy Policy is available online at www.ReaderService.com or upon request from the Harlequin Reader Service. We make a portion of our mailing list available to reputable third parties that offer products we believe may interest you. If you prefer that we not exchange your name with third parties, or if you wish to clarify or modify your communication preferences, please visit us at www.ReaderService.com/consumerschoice or write to us at Harlequin Reader Service Preference Service, P.O. Box 9062, Buffalo, NY 14269. Include your complete name and address.

NO PURCHASE NECESSARY!

(left margin) ▶ Detach card and mail today. No stamp needed. ▶

© 2013 HARLEQUIN ENTERPRISES LIMITED ® and ™ are trademarks owned and used by the trademark owner and/or its licensee. Printed in the U.S.A.

HAR-FM-09/13

Chapter Ten

Tears caught in Pandora's throat. She hadn't realized how much she'd craved his kiss until Calder left her standing dazed and confused. A few years from now—six months from now, she'd have Julia back and everything would change.

"Sorry. Didn't mean to spoil your nice night." Arms crossed, lips pressed tight, he'd become the human equivalent of a moody spring storm.

"Then why the dark look? The one fairly screaming you can't stand the sight of me?"

"You're reading too much into this. I'm regrouping. Trying to keep my distance. You know—like an appropriate boss should." He'd stepped in close again. Close enough for his breath's heat to tickle her upper lip.

If she leaned in a quarter inch, she'd no longer be fantasizing about kissing him but indulging in the real thing. But was she strong enough to continue her fight for her daughter and also abandon herself to another man, even a nice one like Calder?

Summoning her last shred of courage, she asked, "What if right now I need you to be more than a boss?"

He groaned before framing her face with his hands. "Do you have any idea what you do to me?"

The feeling was mutual.

But she'd had enough push-pull. She craved more from this man who'd roared into her life as unexpectedly as a runaway freighter. Meeting him, falling for him, was a game changer. What she felt for him had no rules. Maybe he could even help her in her custody battle.

When Pandora touched her lips to Calder's, she closed her eyes. When he met her kiss with exquisite pressure, she could've wept from dizzying relief. Her whole life up to this moment felt like a spinning coin that had only just settled. Pulse racing, she pressed her hands to Calder's chest, surprised to find his heart racing, too.

He deepened the kiss, sweeping her tongue with his.

She fisted his shirt, holding on for all she was worth.

"Damn...." he said when they stopped for air.

When he released her, she was caught off balance, but he was right there, hands on her arms to steady her and provide balance—only what he had no way of knowing was how much more support he'd unwittingly provided. Since taking this job, everything felt shiny and new. Dreams she'd never thought possible, such as living in a real house and finally regaining custody of her daughter and now, maybe even forming a relationship with a man who didn't hit or yell—all of it was coming true.

Her conscience wouldn't allow her to risk losing it all on a technicality, so she blurted, "I want—*need*—you to know, I used to be an alcoholic. My dad physically abused my mother and I followed the same cycle. One night I left our car's lights on and when the battery died, my husband hit me so hard I spent three days in a coma. I got better and h-he went to prison, but back then, I was all messed up. Making my own living was h-hard and booze made me forget the constant, nagging pressures of medical bills and making rent. Liquor was my only friend. I made horrible choices—did things I'll always regret. But I'm better now. You have to know that with every breath of my being, I want this recovery—this amazing new life to work."

He terrified her by taking a step back. "How long since your last drink?"

"Three years." She needed to tell him about Julia, too, but for her daughter the stakes were too high. Of all her many secrets, Julia was the one she held most dear. As much as she'd grown to adore Quinn and his father, losing them would at least be survivable. To permanently lose custody of Julia was unimaginable. "For that, I alternate between being ashamed and proud. I worked hard to become the woman I am today. Even if you don't approve, I—"

Throughout her speech, she'd managed to hold her tears at bay, but when he stepped toward her, wrapping his strong arms around her, his support was more than she could take.

She broke down—hard.

He held her till she calmed, but then he asked gently, "Are you in AA?"

"Yes—I just haven't felt like I needed regular meetings in a while."

"Does Natalie know?"

Pandora nodded. "I credit her—and a few other people— for saving me. She gave me a second chance and I won't let her down. I did janitorial duties in her day care for a year before she ever let me work with children. Two more years of part-time day care and after-school care before she'd let me even think of applying for a job like yours."

He released a long, slow exhale. "I don't know what to say. On the one hand, you've been amazing with Quinn, on the other…"

"I know." Head bowed, she covered her face with her hands. "But if this—whatever it is—between us hadn't developed, none of what I just shared would matter. Even though she's my friend, Natalie drops by at least once a week to check on me. When I tell you I'm never going back to my old way of life, I mean it. There's truth to the adage of being *scared straight*. I'm living proof."

"I appreciate that." He wouldn't make eye contact with her. "But you have to understand this news is—well, let's just say I had my suspicions about you having been abused, but the rest…"

"If you want me to leave, I will." She raised her chin. For as long as she could remember, she'd considered herself a victim, but no more. She'd made grave errors in judgment, but she refused to live the rest of her life being dictated by them.

After waiting for what felt like forever, with no sounds in the house other than the fire's occasional crackle, he finally slipped his arms around her again. Kissed the crown of her head. "Considering the way my own son entered my life, I'm the last one who should be judging."

Her limbs turned quivery with relief. "Thank you."

He tipped her head back, forcing her to meet his gaze. "I should be thanking you. You've made me rethink the whole family thing."

"Yeah?" Through happy tears, she smiled.

"Yeah. With you," he teased, kissing the tip of her nose, "it might not be so bad."

"How's IT going with the nanny?"

"Huh?" Calder had been so deep in thought over that very subject, he'd forgotten Mason was even in the car. Since it was raining, and Pandora told him she and Quinn had nowhere to go, he'd taken the SUV over his bike. He and Mason were now on their way to lunch. Though it'd been almost a week since Pandora's confession, and life with her and Quinn was growing almost idyllic, he still couldn't get her former addiction out of his head.

"The nanny? Please tell me you had a hot homecoming.

Mine sucked." He made a gagging sound. "Heath left the bologna and mayo out on the counter. Smelled like a rotting corpse."

Not sure he was up for sharing, Calder shrugged. "Mine was good." And by good, he meant over-the-top awesome. Pandora had cleared away the balloons, but the banner still hung. Every time he passed beneath it, the paper clipped his head. But he wasn't complaining. The notion that someone besides his parents had been glad to see him safely home still filled him with quiet awe.

"Yeah? The nanny do anything special for you? Make her meat loaf, then serve it wearing nothing but an apron and her glasses?"

Stopped for a light, Calder shot a sideways glare at his gutter-minded friend. "Remember the speech we had a while back about respecting the nanny?"

"Sure, but you've gotta let me have a little fun. Hell, if you aren't dating her, maybe me or even Cooper might want a go?"

"She's taken." Calder hit the gas too hard when the light changed.

"I'm crushed." Hands mockingly over his heart, Mason angled sideways on his seat. "How long you been keeping this from me?"

"Not long. And nothing's official. But I kissed her. But then…" He shook his head. "Things got complicated."

"Bad in bed?"

"Seriously?" His so-called friend had earned another glare.

"What? I'm on a dry spell. Since we got back, sex is pretty much the only thing on my mind."

"TMI, man." Calder shook his head. "Pandora told me she's a recovering alcoholic."

"And?"

Stopped for another light keeping them from reaching their favorite Chinese buffet, Calder asked, "You don't think that's a big deal?"

"Well, sure, but have you seen her drink?"

"No."

"Then what's the problem? I mean, I don't want to downplay that it's serious, but my old man took a bad spell when I was a kid. My mom passed, and—" as if remembering a time he'd rather forget, Mason glanced out the window "—let's just say we both had a rough time of it. My grandparents stepped in, convinced him to get help, and he hasn't had a drink since. He's everything I could hope for in a dad."

"That's a relief." Calder loosened the death grip he'd had on the wheel. "Pandora's amazing, but alcoholism is one of those things you hear about on TV, but unless you have firsthand experience…" He pulled into the restaurant's lot. "I just wasn't sure what to think."

"My advice?" Mason unlatched his seatbelt. "Relax and enjoy the ride."

"I DON'T KNOW what to bring." Wednesday night, Pandora stared at the meager contents of her closet, then looked to Quinn and his father. Calder sat at the foot of her bed with the baby on his lap. Despite their heated first kiss, by mutual agreement they'd opted to take things slow.

It was a seven-hour drive to the resort where they were meeting his family, so he'd taken Friday off, as well as the entire next week. To say she found the prospect of spending all that time with him exciting was the understatement of the decade.

Calder asked, "When's the last time you went shopping?"

"Can't remember. I get most everything from thrift stores. There are some really great bargains, you just have to look at it like a treasure hunt."

"While we applaud your frugality—" he clapped Quinn's hands "—once we load this guy's twenty pounds of traveling gear, if you want, we can make it to the mall in time to grab you a few things for this fancy resort."

"No." A familiar knot seized her stomach. "What I have will do."

"I didn't say what you have wouldn't be fine, I said let's go play. I thought chicks love that sort of thing."

"I'd rather save money." Was now the time to tell him about Julia? How part of her case file required her to be gainfully employed with the same company for a year, and how she also had to provide a stable housing environment for Julia and prove she'd been there for six months? It took not only time for all this but money. Yes, if she maintained her current course, all was well. If not, she'd once again be in trouble with the courts.

"What do you need to stockpile cash for? I'm not complaining, but the fee the agency charges for your services isn't cheap. You probably have more money than I do."

"I have legal fees, all right?" She hated that her tone grew defensive, but when backed into a corner, she fought.

His pinched expression led to him scratching his head. "I'm sorry. I really don't mean to pry, but what are you paying a lawyer for?"

Heart pounding scary hard, Pandora had trouble finding her next breath. She didn't want to tell Calder about Julia. Not yet. Not like this. But if not now, when?

"Hey…" He set squirming Quinn on the floor, then took her hands in his. "Talk to me. You're white as a ghost."

"I need the money to get my child back, all right? Her name's Julia and I was a textbook example of a lousy parent. I showed up drunk at my first custody hearing. My second, I got so mad I cursed at the judge. I—I—" she covered her face with her hands "—I'm humiliated by the person I used to be.

That Saturday you wondered where I was going? I went to one of my monthly supervised visits. In January, assuming I stay on my present course, they move up to bimonthly. So see? I need every dime I make to get my daughter back." Her throat ached from tears, but she forced herself to be calm. She wasn't the same woman who'd lost her cool in court. "I've been to AA, to anger-management classes and parenting classes and even a financial course to help me make a proper weekly budget. I'm so ready to put all this knowledge to good use. All I need is my child."

Calder had long since released her. His supportive expression had darkened to pressed lips and narrowed eyes. "So in the meantime, you're practicing on mine?"

"It's not like that."

"Then why hide this from me?" He turned his back on her to stare out the window.

"It wasn't relevant."

"Not relevant that here you are, caring for my kid, when you lost your own? What was Natalie thinking even hiring you?"

No longer able to hold back tears, Pandora dashed toward the bathroom for tissues, and in the process nearly tripped over Quinn, who she'd forgotten was crawling on the floor.

The startled infant cried.

She lifted him for a comforting hug, but Calder took his son. "I'm going to need time to process this."

"Please, Calder..." She tried holding his hand, but he pulled away. "Please give me a second chance. Going to jail was the best thing that ever happened to me. It scared me straight. I promise, I—"

"You've been to jail?" He laughed without a trace of humor. "This just keeps getting better. My gut instincts were right about there being something *off* with you. I just didn't know to what degree."

This couldn't be happening.

As if time had dulled to slow motion, Pandora all but fell onto the foot of her bed. She was aware of tears wetting her face, but lacked the strength to do anything but let them fall.

"I'm, ah, going to take Quinn for a ride." The baby had quieted in his father's arms. "We'll be gone for about an hour. I'd appreciate you packing your things and being gone when we return."

"Calder?" With her eyes she begged him to at least look her way, but his only action was to leave the room.

SINCE PANDORA HAD already packed Quinn's diaper bag for their morning drive, Calder suddenly decided to turn toward the interstate that led to the resort his mom and Harold were staying at. He'd experienced pain, but nothing like this. He felt humiliated and embarrassed, yet at the same time a crushing sense of loss for the woman Pandora had spent so much time portraying.

How could he have been so blind?

How could she have been so duplicitous?

Thirty minutes into the drive, Quinn grew fussy.

Calder pulled over at a truck stop to change his son's diaper, struggling with the sticky tabs as usual. Using the bottled water and premeasured formula Pandora had placed amongst Quinn's things, he prepared a quick bottle, then climbed into the backseat to feed his son.

The trip wasn't supposed to be like this.

He'd looked forward to it for over a month. He'd not only been excited to see his mom, but for his mom to see Quinn and to finally meet Pandora, whom he'd talked so much about.

Now? As much as he wanted to see his mother, he dreaded the lecture she'd deliver on how he hadn't done adequate research before even hiring a nanny who had a prison record.

But hadn't Natalie been in charge of all that? Should he sue her agency to protect other unsuspecting parents from Pandora's lies?

Had she lied? his conscience probed. Or had she omitted? Did the technicality matter?

This was why Calder had protected himself all these years from entering any sort of relationship. They were doomed to fail. His dad had been married so many times Calder doubted he could even name all his in-laws. Sure, Calder's mom was happy, but at what cost? His dad put her through hell.

Quinn finished his bottle and drifted off to sleep.

Calder eased him back into his safety seat, then resumed his drive. He'd like a nap himself, except he feared dreaming of Pandora, so he didn't dare close his eyes.

"Honey, it's okay...."

At Natalie's homey ranch-style house, Pandora had blown her nose so many times it felt raw. She knew her friend meant well, but she also knew nothing would be okay. "You say that, but you know part of my Social Services agreement is to maintain the same child-appropriate address for six months *and* have a job. Now I have neither. I'll never get Julia back."

"Hey, now. Try not to worry." Natalie patted Pandora's knee before rising. "I'm making more tea. Any particular flavor request?"

"Tea won't help."

Frozen, eyebrows raised, Natalie asked, "You're not thinking of drinking away your fears?"

"No. *Lord, no.* And it hurts me you'd even think such a thing."

"Sorry. Guess I'm in kind of a panic, too." She leaned against the kitchen wall. "Don't take this the wrong way, but maybe I messed up by even suggesting you for that job."

Pandora looked at her friend a good long while, then

began gathering her purse and the sole suitcase holding all her clothes.

Losing Calder before she'd ever really had him hurt enough. To hear the woman she respected above all others still doubting her was too much.

"You're taking that wrong." Natalie chased her to the door. "I meant I should've protected your past by keeping you on at the day care. No one asks questions there. All they see is you doing a great job."

"Please move."

Natalie blocked her home's entry. "Don't go. Not like this."

"I'm fine." Pandora gently nudged her friend aside. "I'll be even better on my own."

CALDER HAD BEEN on the road a good two hours when his cell rang. *Pandora?*

The dash's caller ID read Natalie Lawrence. Usually when he'd spoken with her, she phoned from her agency—Earth Angels.

"Hello?"

"Calder—I'm glad I found you. Have you seen Pandora?"

"No. I left with Quinn a while ago."

"And she hasn't called?" Was there worry in her tone? He shouldn't care, but he did. In the time it'd taken him to recover from the shock of just how much of her past Pandora had kept from him, he'd seen her silence for what it had been—a defensive maneuver. Regardless, he couldn't have a former criminal caring for his child.

Is that really the reason you're shunning her? Or is it something more? Like you were in too deep, too fast, and her shady past gave you the perfect escape?

"I haven't heard from her." Calder tightened his grip on the wheel. "But she's a big girl. I'm sure she's okay."

"Did she even tell you half of what her ex put her through? She almost died. He's in jail for attempted murder."

An empathetic pang tore through him. "I'm sorry. That doesn't excuse what she did." Out of sheer morbid curiosity, he asked, "What landed her in jail?"

There was a long pause.

"Natalie?"

"Crack cocaine. She was arrested for possession in a sting operation. She claims it was the first and last time she ever used."

Chest tight with frustration, he asked, "You believe her?"

"Yes." Another pause. "Even if she lied about that, there's no way she isn't living her true life now. She's clean. If I thought for one second she wasn't, I never would've linked my own reputation with hers."

In the time she'd lived in Calder's home, Pandora had managed to add to her financial safety net. Trouble was, that money had been earmarked for legal fees, but more important, her own home—at the very least a nice apartment. As she hadn't yet raised enough for either, she spent a listless night in a cheap motel. Between throbbing bass, breaking glass and a couple fights, it was a wonder she ever drifted off to sleep.

She woke at 5:00 a.m. confused about where she was.

It took a few seconds for the previous night to come rushing back. A few seconds more to find enough composure to not surrender to more tears.

She wasn't hungry, but coffee sounded good.

Maybe if she forced down an egg and toast her head would be clear enough to choose her next move.

Remembering an all-night diner on the corner, she grabbed her coat, purse and room key, opening the door with the chain lock still in place to have a peek outside.

Places like this used to be the norm for her. Now this world felt frightening and alien.

Finding the motel parking lot clear of anything but cars as crappy as hers, she ventured outside, careful to make sure her door was locked behind her. The restaurant was within easy walking distance, so she set off through misty fog made all the more eerie by the motel sign's blinking red-neon glow.

Almost to the diner's door, she got a shock when a scantily dressed teenage girl stepped out from a narrow alley. A much older man followed, tucking in his shirt. The implications made Pandora's stomach roil. But then at her worst, how many nights had she been tempted to do the same—not even for money, but a measly fifth of vodka?

The teen caught Pandora staring. "What're you lookin' at, bitch?"

Ignoring her, Pandora hastened her pace until she reached the diner's overly warm interior.

The place was surprisingly crowded with patrons who she guessed from their jeans and uniformed shirts were factory workers.

"Sit wherever you like!" shouted a waitress from behind a counter.

Pandora found a corner booth.

She looked out the window, but as it was still dark, all she saw was her own reflection. Behind her glasses, her red-rimmed eyes appeared hollow. Dark shadows had formed underneath. She'd long since lost her ponytail, and her long hair hung dirty and wild. She hadn't looked this bad since the night of her mug shot.

"Coffee?" The waitress startled her. "Sorry. Didn't mean to sneak up on you. Rough night?"

Pandora half laughed. "You could say that."

The woman glanced over her shoulder. "Boss would have

my ass for asking, but if you need a little, you know, pick-me-up? I've got most anything you crave."

"Um, I'm okay. Thanks. Just coffee, please."

"You got it."

Pandora wanted so badly to stay strong, but for the first time in she couldn't remember when she'd lost her will to fight. With no job and no place to live there was no way she'd get Julia back.

Natalie might not have technically let her go, but her words refused to leave Pandora's head. *Don't take this the wrong way, but maybe I messed up by even suggesting you for that job.*

If that was how her friend honestly felt, Pandora had too much pride to go back.

Then there was Calder. His kiss.

The waitress's offer intruded on everything else.

...If you need a little, you know, pick-me-up? I've got most anything you crave.

Oh, did Pandora crave.

Chapter Eleven

"I don't even know what to say."

"Not much to say." Saturday morning, Calder topped off his mom's coffee from the carafe room service had left with their breakfast. Harold, his stepdad, had already left for his day's meetings. Calder had spent the past thirty minutes filling his mom in on Pandora's past.

He'd left out their kiss.

That part was too private. Too raw.

Quinn fussed on his grandmother's lap. The poor little guy hadn't been himself since leaving home.

"You can't be cranky when you're with Nana." His mom adopted a singsong tone.

Quinn wasn't having it and broke into a full-on wail.

"Let me take him." Calder reached for his son but didn't have much better luck calming him.

"Hmm…" His mom rested her elbows on the table, framing her mug with both hands. "Do you suppose he misses Pandora?"

"I'm sure he's just hungry."

"I fed him a bottle right before you got up."

Great. There went that theory. Calder checked his son's diaper to find that hope blown, too.

"I can't believe I'm even saying this," Gloria said, "but maybe you overreacted. Your uncle Pete drank and Aunt Melanie's son—you know? Ulie? Well, he was a raging pothead in college. Of course, he's better now—a lawyer in Boston. Your aunt's very proud. So, see? People can make mistakes and get better."

He sighed. "She was in prison, Mom."

"Prison or jail? There is a difference."

Quinn cried harder.

His mom stood, taking the infant. She paced, all the while singing "You Are My Sunshine" in a soft, lyrical tone. The song took him back to his childhood. To when he'd had a bad day at school and he'd come home to her hugs and fresh-baked chocolate-chip cookies.

Quinn finally calmed.

The relief from his crying struck Calder as profound.

Calder said, "You were a good mom. Still are. I'm sorry for what Dad put you through."

She waved off his concern. "That was a million years ago. And while I love you for thinking of me, would it shock you to know I was secretly relieved your father cheated?"

"What?" Calder narrowed his eyes. "That's crazy."

"No, hon, it's called we got married way too young, and I fell for your dad's Paul McCartney imitation but pretty much couldn't stand anything else about him. We worked in the bedroom, but nowhere—"

"Stop." He waved his hands. "I don't wanna hear this."

"You need to hear it." She set Quinn in the portable hotel crib, along with a few toys. "I've been afraid for a while now that you've never gotten serious about a woman because of the example your father and I set. This Pandora intrigues me. You've never spoken to me about a woman the way you did her."

"It wasn't like that between us." He sat at the foot of the bed, trying not to think about the fact that had he never insisted they go to a mall, Pandora would be here with him now. They'd have all shared a meal, maybe spent the afternoon hiking or riding bikes down one of the resort trails.

That was a first—lying to his mother.

"It's okay, you know?" Her arm around his shoulder, she joined him on the bed. "If you did have feelings for the nanny? Sounds fun to me—like the kind of romance you'd see in a chick flick."

He groaned, covering his face with his hands. "All right, so what if it was like that? And she *is* fully recovered? Then I'm the one who's messed up."

"Then I'd say if you stand a chance of wooing her back into your life, you've got work to do."

"THANK YOU FOR seeing me on such short notice." Pandora followed her caseworker into her cubicle. It was Monday. A cold rain had settled in and she felt chilled to her core.

"I'm glad I had time. Please—" Fran gestured to her guest chair "—have a seat."

Pandora did. Her palms were so sweaty, she pressed them to her knees, willing her legs not to do their usual nervous jiggle.

"How can I help you?"

"You know how hard I've been working to regain custody of Julia, right?"

Fran smiled. "In all my years on this job, I don't think I've ever seen anyone work as diligently as you. Not only have you excelled in all state-sponsored parenting classes, but your performance at the day care has been truly remarkable. I had misgivings about you taking the nanny position, but, if anything, you've proved you're ready to resume caring for Julia. By your March hearing, assuming you maintain status quo, I'll wholeheartedly recommend your full parental rights be returned."

"Th-that's just it...." Pandora's stomach churned as if she'd come down with a terrible case of throw-up flu. "I want to be totally up-front with you. Friday, my, um, direct employer, Mr. Remington, released me from my duty of watching his son."

"You mean you were fired?" The caseworker dug through a stack for Pandora's file, then made a notation.

"Yes, ma'am."

"On what grounds?"

"I—I told him about my past problems with alcohol. And about my daughter. And jail."

"I see…." More notes written. Pandora didn't hear the scratch of pencil lead against paper but nails in her coffin. "So you failed to tell him when you were first hired?"

"Well, since I got the job through the Earth Angel agency—" she clasped her hands so hard on her lap that she dug her fingernails into the backs of them "—I assumed he would've asked any questions at the agency office."

Fran nodded. "And what does the agency say about all this? I was under the impression the owner—" she flipped through several pages "—Natalie Lawrence, felt you'd done an exemplary job with all your assignments? Did she also release you from duty?"

"Honestly?" Moments earlier Pandora had been cold, but she was now hot. Resisting the urge to claw at the neck of her sweater, she said, "I haven't spoken with Natalie since Friday. I was so upset, I wanted to see you first—assure you I will find another job and adequate housing."

"Pandora…" Setting the file on her desk, Fran sighed. "You've been with the agency for three solid years. My advice? Go to Natalie and ask her to return you to your previous work in the day care. Unless there's more you're not telling me, I see nothing here in your file that would indicate she wouldn't have you back. Would you like me to call?"

"No, ma'am. I'll do it." Head bowed, Pandora accepted the

fact that yet again she'd be swallowing her pride. For Julia, she'd do it all day long. "But I'm worried about the housing portion of my case plan. It requires me to have lived at the same address for six months. The fact that I will no longer live in the same household where I worked means that by the time of my hearing, even if I find an apartment today, I'll have only lived there four months."

"I see where that could be a problem." Tapping the file with her pencil, Fran said, "You've been frank with me, so I'll return the favor. Most times, the judges who handle our cases want to return children to their parents. That's the primary goal of our job. That said, though you're an exemplary mom now, you and I both know that hasn't always been the case."

Pandora nodded, biting her lower lip to keep from crying.

"In fact, early on, you were one of the most challenging cases I've ever had."

"I—I know. And I'm sorry."

"Don't be sorry." Fran set her pencil on her desk, then leaned forward, taking Pandora's hands. "What I need you to do is secure a suitable place for you and Julia to potentially live—like, yesterday. Assuming you stay with the agency and have no other problems by March, I'll do my best to smooth things over with the judge."

"Thank you," Pandora said. *"Thank you."*

"Don't thank me yet. You've still got work to do, and when it comes to judges, please realize I don't have a magic wand."

PANDORA LEFT SOCIAL SERVICES and drove straight to Earth Angels.

While Natalie was in an appointment with a potential new client Pandora made small talk with Anna, who handled payroll.

The moment the client was gone, Pandora winced when her friend grabbed her by the arm, yanking her into her office before closing the door. "Where have you been? I've been worried sick! And when are you getting a cell?"

"First, I'm staying at the Super 9 off the interstate. Second, I'm sorry I worried you, but you really hurt my feelings. Third, I refuse to spend one dime on anything other than making a stable home for Julia and me."

Shaking her head, Natalie joined Pandora on the sofa and took a bag from the coffee table. "I figured you'd say that about the phone, which is why I bought you this." She handed over the gift. "I literally haven't slept the whole time you've been gone. Open it."

It was a GoPhone.

"No contracts or anything. I put sixty minutes' worth of calling cards in there, too, so you have no excuse not to let me know what's going on with you."

Sighing, Pandora said, "Thanks, but you do realize I'm not twelve?"

"Yes. But do you realize just how much you mean not only to me, but to Fran and Anna and lots of other people whose lives you've touched? Fran called—she wanted me to reassure her you were still gainfully employed."

"What'd you say?"

"Of course." Natalie winked. "Doris called in sick today, so you're desperately needed in the three-year-old room. After that, I've circled a half-dozen apartments for us to check out."

That familiar knot formed in her throat as Pandora asked, "Why are you doing all this?"

"Simple." Natalie crushed her in a hug. "You're my best friend."

WHILE HIS MOM took care of Quinn, Calder ran until his lungs burned from crisp morning mountain air. Then he ran more. Until he couldn't hear Pandora crying. See the pain in her eyes.

He'd made a mistake kissing her.

Leaves crunching beneath his feet, Calder ignored what under ordinary circumstances would've been an awesome panoramic view. If he'd kept things professional between him and Pandora, would her past have mattered as much? He wouldn't have taken what she'd done personally. He wouldn't have wished he'd met her in high school, saving her the pain of ever having been hurt. He wouldn't wonder about her little girl—if she shared her mom's pretty smile. Most of all, he wouldn't blame himself for quite possibly being the one who pushed her back over that alcohol ledge.

But then, how egotistical was he to assume he even had that power? No doubt Pandora was fine. And if she had returned to drinking, that only proved him right and she shouldn't be around his son.

And if she hadn't? And she really was all she'd portrayed herself to be? That meant his commitment issues were as real as the disease she'd once battled.

"Whoa!" Calder damn near mowed his stepfather down. Harold wore his business-casual clothes and had been headed to the conference center.

"Sorry."

"That's okay," Harold said with a wry smile. "Your mom filled me in on your nanny problems. I imagine your mind was on that. Ask me, you dodged a potential bullet. A man can't be too safe when it comes to protecting his family."

Calder reveled in this vindication. "See? That's what I thought, but Mom says I shouldn't have let her go." He couldn't even bring himself to say Pandora's name. "She thinks I have the problem, and then gave me a ridiculous lecture on how she's worried her and Dad's divorce emotionally scarred me for life."

Harold glanced at his watch. "I'm seriously late for this

morning's session. How about I skip it altogether and we grab the breakfast of champions?"

"What's that?"

On their way toward the main lodge, Harold patted him on the back. "Bloody Marys followed by a truckload of bacon and a biscuit-and-gravy chaser—only don't tell your mom. My cholesterol's already through the roof."

By the time they'd finished their meal, Calder was reminded how much he enjoyed his stepdad's company. His real dad may not have always been there for him, but for as long as he could remember, Harold had.

"Thanks, man."

"For what?" His stepdad finished his drink.

"You know—being around. You're a good guy, and best as I can remember, I wasn't exactly fun to deal with."

Harold laughed. "Not gonna lie—there were times you were a mouthy handful, but all in all, your mom and I couldn't be prouder."

"What do you think of Mom's worry that I have *problems* when it comes to dealing with women?"

After signaling for another drink, Harold said, "We could be here all day discussing women and their problems. Way I see it, once you find the right lady, everything else sorts itself out."

Leaning forward, Calder realized a sense of urgency had taken hold. "How do you know if a woman's *right?*"

"From my experience, you just know. To this day, I remember your mom coming into my office with you in tow. She and your father had just broken up and I remember thinking how brave she was—a single woman raising her child. But she gave me the most beautiful smile…" He downed more of his drink. "Don't mean to get all sappy on you, but *you know when you know.* For me, your mom's smile stopped time. Anyway, she wanted to invest her divorce settlement and I was more than happy to help. Whenever she was in the office, she brought you along. You were eight and you refused to sit in any chair. You always wanted to be under your chair, driving Matchbox cars. I'll never forget the first time I showed up at your house to take your mom on a date—you asked if she was now going to cheat on you with me." He shook his head. "For the longest time, you saw me as a threat." His eyes shone and he patted his chest. "Meant the world when you finally let me in. I—I couldn't have kids of my own, so I mean it when I tell you that in every sense of the word, I view you as mine. I loved every one of your Little League games and Boy Scout meetings. When you went off to visit your dad, I worried you wouldn't want to come home."

Calder wasn't sure how to process this information. All this time he'd had a great father, but he'd been too self-absorbed to see Harold for what he'd been—a devoted family man who'd been a faithful, loving friend to him and a great husband to Calder's mom for twenty years. So why did Calder identify more with his cheating birth father than the true father who'd always been there for him?

For all these years, why had Calder assumed he was incapable of commitment when it turned out he'd had the perfect family role models all along?

And what was wrong with him that when it came to women, he couldn't get it right? More specifically, when Pandora shared her story, why hadn't he listened instead of driving her away?

A ROACH SCURRIED across the counter where Pandora had set her purse. She snatched her bag from the cracked and stained beige surface. Would any amount of bleach return it to life?

"It's close to work," Natalie said with forced cheer.

"It also reeks of the former tenant's cigarettes and I'm pretty sure the carpet's *crunching* beneath my feet."

"I don't know…" Arms crossed, Natalie appraised the shadowy living room with its one cell-like window. "If you add curtains and lots of plants, the place has potential."

Pandora sighed. "I appreciate your upbeat attitude, but this is the fourth apartment we've seen and they're all overpriced."

"How about you move in with me?" Natalie suggested. "I have room. You're more than welcome to pay loads of rent, which I will save for you, me and Julia to take a trip to Walt Disney World, then we'll all live happily ever after—assuming I haven't met a man before turning eighty." She sat on the arm of a sagging brown sofa.

"You think we need men to be happy? Obviously, marriage didn't work out for me, and here I finally thought I might have something real with Calder, only to have that blow up, too." She raked her hair into a ponytail, securing it with an elastic band from her purse. "I'm done."

"I'm not quite ready to give up altogether," Natalie said, "but after what Calder put you through, I respect the fact you are. The thing is, you're even younger than me. You never know where life may take you—so what do you say, wanna be my roomie?"

Pandora had to follow her instincts on this. "I can't tell you how much your offer means, but I want a place of my own not only for the judge who reviews my case, but for Julia. I need to prove I'm not just a good mom but a great one."

"Aw…" Eyes shining, Natalie left her perch to wrap Pandora in a hug. "Sweetie, haven't you already proved yourself just by making it past this mess with Calder only to come out stronger on the other end?"

"I did, didn't I?" Pandora couldn't help but smile. "Did I tell you one morning at breakfast, a waitress offered items that weren't on the menu? For a split second I was tempted, but one vision of Julia's face was all I needed to politely decline."

"I'm so proud of you. Geez, you should be proud of yourself."

Pandora was. She just wished another part of her didn't regret not having earned Calder's approval.

"I CAN'T BELIEVE this is our last night here." Even at their table in the resort's main dining room, Calder's mom held Quinn on her lap. "I'm going to miss this angel."

Harold said, "Without a nanny, Calder's going to need help. How about you stay with him another week or two?"

"That'd be great." Calder climbed right aboard that bandwagon. "You'd not only spare me the long drive home alone, but I obviously need help selecting Quinn's new nanny."

"If I didn't know better—" she landed an elbow's to her husband's ribs "—I'd think you're trying to get rid of me."

"Never, sweetheart." Harold put his arm around her shoulders, then gave her a kiss. When Calder had been a kid, that sort of thing grossed him out. Now? He found comfort in the fact that his mom had a great guy.

As for Calder finding a great gal?

He figured the lingering ache in his chest told him he already had but had let her get away.

"THIS IS REALLY NICE." Thursday afternoon, Pandora turned in a slow circle, taking in the garage apartment's leafy view. There were two bedrooms and though the honey-toned wood floor was scuffed from years of use and the yellow walls had faded, they were yellow, and Pandora took that as a good sign. Tall, paned windows overlooked the main home's shady backyard, and in exchange for gathering mail and watching pets while the owners frequently traveled, the rent was ridiculously low.

"No kidding," Natalie said. "Maybe I need to move?"

Pandora gave her friend's arm a playful swat. "Don't even think about it. This place is mine."

After checking out the rest of the apartment and especially admiring the claw-foot tub, Pandora met with the owner in the main house's kitchen, proudly signing a six-month lease, then providing her first and last month's rent in cash. She still had enough in savings to cover at least two more months and purchase a few furnishings at yard sales and thrift stores.

"That felt good," Pandora said once she and Natalie were back in the car with a brand-new set of apartment keys. "I'm doing this. Just like we talked about in all my parenting classes, I'm supporting myself and soon my daughter and it's not scary but empowering."

"I'm so glad for—uh-oh…." Natalie had taken her phone from her purse and was now checking messages. "What's wrong?"

"I have a message from Calder."

Chapter Twelve

Calder left a message for Natalie's cell, then turned off his phone. To his mom, he asked, "You don't suppose she's purposely not answering?"

"You're losing it." She stood at the kitchen sink peeling carrots.

Quinn seemed happy to be home and tooled about in his walker.

"Stranger things could happen."

"You're giving yourself too much credit. From everything you've told me about Pandora and her friend Natalie, both are strong, capable women fully able to breathe without you. If Natalie's any kind of businesswoman, she'll return your call within an hour."

Damn, Calder hated it when his mother was right.

Sure enough, just as he'd taken the rake and a few trash bags from the garage, his cell rang—this time with the familiar Earth Angels number.

After a few minutes of painfully awkward chitchat, he got to the point. "Look, the reason I called is that I want to talk to Pandora. Any idea where she is?"

After a long pause, she said, "Yes. I know exactly where she is. I also know she has no interest in speaking with you. She's doing great, Calder—better than ever. You firing her only made her stronger."

"I'm glad." He truly was. Only, her success proved him an even bigger ass where she was concerned. "So how about you tell her I called, then let her decide whether or not she wants to talk?"

"Ever occur to you she already has your number? Trust me, if she had any interest in reconnecting, she'd have already made the first move."

Calder tried another route. "What if I want to rehire her?"

"Sorry, but I won't send you anyone else. If you don't trust my judgment in only hiring top-notch nannies, then I no longer trust you to treat them in a professional, respectful manner. As far as I'm concerned, Mr. Remington, you're blackballed from the Earth Angels agency."

When she hung up, it took every shred of Calder's self-control not to throw his phone.

His mother asked, "What'd she say?"

"Mind watching Quinn? I need to run an errand."

"Of course I'll watch him, but first tell me what that was all about."

"Mom…" He kissed her forehead. "That was about Pandora's friend Natalie launching a battle. What she doesn't know is I excel at war."

"Not to interfere in your business, but, hon, I thought the whole purpose of your call was to find peace?"

PANDORA WAS ABLE to move in immediately, and just as soon as she hefted all seven of her boxes filled with personal belongings—a marked increase from her previous five—up the stairs, leaving them in the middle of the living room floor, she called Fran from the phone Natalie had given her, leaving her a message about her new address and number.

Finished with that vital task, she took a moment to wander around her new space. Partially furnished, it had a sort of shabby-chic appeal she couldn't wait to embellish with yard-sale finds. In what would be Julia's room, she imagined the sun-flooded space as the quintessential little-girl's room. The twin bed made with a girlie floral, ruffled spread. Lots of cozy, colorful throw pillows and stuffed animals. Maybe a rag rug she'd spend cold winter nights crafting.

In her own room, she made her bed. Her comforter and sheets matched the faded-yellow walls, and her linens smelled fresh from the washing she'd given them while at Natalie's.

She hung her towels in the bathroom and arranged her books on the built-in shelves flanking the brick fireplace.

There were loads of items she'd need to shop for. Plates and silverware. Pots and pans. All were available for next to nothing at thrift stores. She'd take her time, carefully picking exactly what she wanted.

Funny, when Calder had sent her packing, she'd felt nearly as low as the night she'd landed in jail. She'd felt as if everything she'd worked for had been lost. But now she was almost grateful for what he'd done. He'd given her the gift of recognizing her own power and self-worth. He'd shown her she could not only survive on her own but thrive. One day soon, she and Julia would get along just fine without a man.

Even if that first kiss she'd shared with Calder had been magical and each one after even better, she was done mourning what might've been. From here, she vowed to only look forward.

And if her thoughts occasionally strayed to Calder?

Well, she'd view what they'd briefly shared as a lovely, never fully realized dream.

"You did it!" Pandora said to three-year-old Rose, who'd just written *H, I* and *J* with her chubby index finger on a cookie sheet filled with sand. Lots of times students used crayons or fat markers, but having children correlate writing not only with tools but their hands helped reinforce the whole concept.

"I smart!" Rose beamed up at her, and as much as Pandora missed working with Quinn, for the past few days she'd enjoyed working with slightly older kids.

"You sure are. Now I want you to see Miss Donna at the Magic Marker station. She's going to let you pick your favorite color to use next."

"Okay." The girl ambushed Pandora in a hug. "Thank you, Miss *Pannora.*"

"You're very welcome."

Billy was next in line at Pandora's station. "Hi, sweetie. Do you remember how to use hand sanitizer?"

"Yeah, but it smells bad."

"I'm sorry." Lowering her voice to a whisper, she asked, "Know what?"

He shook his head.

"I don't like it, either. But we need to keep our sand nice and clean so everyone can have a turn. Can you think of a way to get your hands nice and clean without using the goopy sanitizer stuff?"

Nose scrunched, he took a second to think about it. "Wash with soap?"

"You're right." She gave his nose a playful tweak. "How'd you get so smart?"

Grinning, he said, "Mommy says I got her brain and Daddy's poop!"

"Oh?" Kids really did say the darnedest things, and this was one of those times. "Maybe what your mom really meant was that you're as smart as your mom and as handsome as your dad?"

"Nope," he said with a firm shake of his head. "She said Dad's poop!"

"Wow, okay, well, let's wash our hands and in the future not talk about bathroom things unless we're in the bathroom."

While Billy ran to the sink station, Pandora used a hand

brush and dustpan to sweep sand that had fallen on the floor. Feeling a tingling on her neck, she glanced over her shoulder to see Calder.

She jolted upright so fast she hit her head on the table.

A dozen curses shot through her throbbing head, but considering her ultra-G-rated setting, she bit her lower lip instead and rubbed the spot where it hurt.

Calder was instantly at her side, helping her back into her chair. She was now stuck trying to ignore the way the simplest touch of his hand on her elbow ignited her longing for him all over again. "You okay?"

"Fine." If anything, having him near made her heart hurt worse than her head. Her pulse raced uncomfortably and her mouth had gone dry. "What're you doing here?"

"Miss Pandora?" Billy returned from the hand-washing station, only he'd forgotten to use his towel, so he dripped all over the sand. Wide-eyed, he looked at a towering Calder. "Is he a stranger danger?"

Yes! "No, sweetie. Just someone I know." Forcing her runaway heart to slow, she said, "Could you please dry between your fingers so we don't get our sand any more wet?"

"Oops. I forgot!" He was off in a flash, giving Pandora about thirty seconds to get rid of Calder.

"I'm glad I found you." He pulled over one of the miniature toddler chairs. He looked ridiculous seated on it, but at least he was now closer to eye level. "We need to talk."

"Why?"

A muscle ticked in his clenched jaw. "Don't play games. I hate the way we left things."

"We didn't leave anything, Calder. You told me to get out of your house, so I did. End of story."

"Is this enough?" Billy returned, wriggling his now-dry fingers.

"Perfect." Pandora took the child's arm, drawing him back

onto his chair. "Now, remember how to make the letters *H, I* and *J?*"

"I think so." His brow furrowed with concentration.

Pandora found herself resenting Calder's intrusion. He may not see it, but her job was important. Just as she'd made a difference in Quinn's life, she was doing the same for her new charges.

"Good, sweetie. Whenever you're ready, give it a try."

"Pandora, please…" Calder got up from the chair and knelt next to her, his breath warm in her ear. Every wary, weary inch of her hungered for him, yet self-protective instincts kicked in, reminding her the second she'd let down her guard he'd hurt her once and surely would again. "I see you're busy now, but where are you staying? With Natalie? Give me her address and I'll stop by after work."

"The fact that you don't think me capable of finding my own place to stay speaks volumes."

"Miss Pandora?" Billy looked up at her. "Am I doing it right?"

"Just about perfect, sweetheart. Only, I want you to wipe out what you have and try again. This time make your *H* a little fatter."

"Okay!"

"I know I screwed up," Calder whispered for only her to hear. The sincerity of his words, the faint trace of coffee lacing his warm breath, proved her undoing.

She opened Billy's report file, removed one of the blank pages then wrote her new address. "Come over at six. Please bring Quinn. I miss him something fierce."

"He misses you, too."

"Miss Pandora, can you make the H for me?"

"Sure, sweetie." She wiped out what he'd done, then drew him an example. "How about you draw three of them right next to mine. Can you do that?"

"I think so…."

With Billy refocused on his task, she returned her attention to Calder. "You need to leave."

"Sure." As quietly as he'd arrived, Calder was gone.

Pandora hated herself for already missing him.

Above all, she reminded herself nothing mattered more than bringing her daughter home.

"WELL?" CALDER'S MOM all but pounced on him the second he walked through his door. She was still in the kitchen, only this time washing bottles. "Was she there?"

"Oh—she was not only there, but working so patiently with some little kid she looked like a saint."

"She hadn't been drinking? Or God forbid, worse?"

Was it wrong he shot his mom a dirty look? Her question made him feel foolish. "No. She was the same uber-responsible child-care giver I've known. No trace of the druggie I basically accused her of being."

"Good. Never have I been happier to see you proved wrong. And since I'm on a roll, while you were gone, I got to thinking about how much time I've seen you put in with Quinn and I've reached a decision."

"Yeah?" He opened the fridge and grabbed a couple slices of bologna. With his mom temporarily caring for the baby, and once he patched things up with Pandora, she'd no doubt move back in and his life would be on track.

"As much as I love being with my grandson, I think it's you who truly needs to be with him."

"What're you talking about? I'm with him all the time."

"Really? Then how much formula do you use to make a bottle? Do you know what types of foods he's supposed to eat? What happens if he starts crying and won't stop?"

"That doesn't happen."

"Gee, could that be because either Pandora or I have always been around to buffer you from actually knowing your son?"

Heels of his hands pressed to his forehead, Calder asked, "What is this? National Rag on Calder Day?"

"I'm not *ragging* on you, hon, but trying to teach you to be a better father. Just a guess, but I think you were so quick to jump on Pandora because her faults made your own not look so bad. What you don't get is that your lack of connection with Quinn will have lasting results. Don't believe me? Look at your relationship with your father, then tell me how good you are at relationships."

THE WHOLE RIDE to Pandora's new place, Calder wanted to be angry with his mom but couldn't. She'd added vital pieces to his own personal puzzle. The one thing he disagreed with was that he didn't actively participate in Quinn's everyday care.

Hell, he changed diapers. Gave baths. And what was the point of memorizing formula-to-water ratios when they were written on the side of the formula can?

Knowing Pandora's concerns about money, he was afraid she was living in a seedy part of town. What he found himself driving through was a neighborhood far nicer than his own. He knew it was the historic Ghent district but had never paid much attention to the homes—just bars.

The address Pandora gave him turned out to be a full-on Tudor mansion complete with its own small forest protected by ivy-covered, brick walls. Her apartment was above a four-car garage. Age-old servants' quarters?

He parked his SUV, grabbed Quinn and his gear from the back, then mounted the stairs, eager to apologize and get Pandora back to living with him. This place was nice and all, but she belonged at his house.

Hand poised to knock, nerves seized his stomach.

What should he say? It wasn't like him to not have a plan.

At work, he had everything figured out, but when it came to Pandora—even his son—he was a wreck.

She opened her door. The mere sight of her took his breath away. She wasn't wearing her glasses, which made her green eyes all the more striking. Her long, dark hair hung wavy and loose. He remembered holding her, burying his face in that hair, breathing in her sweet floral shampoo. He craved her smile, but instead of gifting it to him, she reserved it only for his son.

Quinn squealed and laughed, holding out his arms and pinching his fingers.

"Hey, handsome! There's my precious boy. Look how big you are!" Pandora took the squirming boy from Calder's arms.

While his son and Pandora got reacquainted, Calder sat on the plaid sofa, feeling about as needed as mosquitoes at a barbecue.

Quinn's smile was so big he drooled.

Of course, Pandora was first on the scene with a dishcloth to wipe him clean.

Calder didn't think of himself as the jealous type, but seeing how much his own son preferred Pandora's company to his rammed home his mom's earlier rant. He truly didn't have a meaningful relationship with Quinn. The knowledge not only hurt but left him more than a little ashamed and confused as to what he was supposed to do about it.

Eyeing a plate filled with neatly sliced cheese and summer sausage circled by crackers, Calder helped himself. Since the woman he'd come to see was ignoring him, he might as well do something with his time.

"Pout much?" Pandora asked. Still-smiley Quinn rode on her hip, grabbing her hair.

"That's stupid. I don't pout."

She laughed. "Look in the mirror."

He growled.

Seated in an armchair opposite him, holding Quinn's hands while jiggling him on her knee, she asked, "Is he walking yet?"

"Nope."

"Said any recognizable words?"

"Not that I've heard."

"I thought he was getting close." She fussed with Quinn's fine hair. "Seems like ages since I've seen him."

"That's why I'm here."

"Oh?" She still had eyes only for Quinn.

Regardless, Calder forged on. "First things first—I owe you an apology. Your confession scared me. I should've given it a while to sink in, thinking about the person you've become rather than giving you a knee-jerk reaction."

She said nothing. Just sat there, holding Quinn's hands, inspecting his little fingers.

"So I was thinking, with that out of the way, let's get your gear packed and we'll have you back in your old room in under an hour. My mom's still here until the morning, so I'll take both my girls out for a nice steak dinner. It'll be fun."

"Are you even listening to yourself? You sound like the one who may be drunk."

"What's that mean?" He sat forward, resting his elbows on his knees.

"It means you're crazy if you think I want anything to do with you."

"I know you don't mean that, any more than I meant to send you away."

"But you did." Her pretty, green eyes welled with tears. "And it hurt."

He slid off the sofa, shoved the coffee table aside to kneel before her for the second time that day. Taking her hands, he said, "I screwed up, okay? I'm sorry. But you have to understand how much you caught me off guard. Jail? Losing your child? Those are some pretty major bombs. What was I supposed to think?"

"I know it sounds bad—it *was* bad. But that's not who I am anymore. I don't like even thinking about those times, so why would I want to talk about them?"

"I get that, but can you understand my shock? I thought we were building something special."

"We are—*were*." She tried covering her face with her hands, but he still had hold of her and drew them down.

"Look at me." He gave her what he hoped was a reassuring squeeze. "I'm sorry. You once asked me for a second chance and I denied you. Well, now it's me needing your generosity, Pandora. Please, come back to my house. Without you…" He bowed his head. "It stopped feeling like a home. *Please.*"

After what seemed like a lifetime of waiting, she finally took a deep breath, then softly answered, "I'm sorry…but no."

Chapter Thirteen

Pandora thrust Quinn at Calder, then dashed to the bathroom.

Emotions—ugly and raw—had balled in her chest, threatening her ability to breathe. Why did Calder affect her like this? Why had she given him so much power?

He banged on the door. "Pandora? Please, let me in."

She wanted to—figuratively and literally.

"I ambushed you like I was storming an enemy camp. I didn't mean it. You may not have noticed, but when it comes to women, I'm not exactly the sharpest tool in the shed."

The fact that he'd even acknowledged such a thing softened her frustration. As for her heart? Where she'd once opened it wide for him, like a rose spreading its petals toward the sun, she was now emotionally exhausted. Torn down and beaten and more than a little confused.

"Forget I asked you to move back in with me—us. How about you come to dinner? Do me the honor of meeting my mom? We'll figure out the rest from there."

She turned to the door, curving her hand around the crystal knob. Forehead resting against the varnished wood planks, she searched her heart for an answer, but only found images of his smile after he'd taken his first bite of her late-night meat-loaf sandwich. Her mind's eye saw him excited to witness her first time touching her toes in the Atlantic. She recalled how much fun they'd had painting her room and the kitchen. How patient he'd been when she'd needed his help that first day at the grocery store. How deeply he'd been touched his first time pushing Quinn on a swing. Most of all, she remembered that first kiss.

The kiss that even now she felt all the way from her tingling lips to her toes.

Against her better judgment, she turned the doorknob, letting Calder not only into the room but her heart.

He held Quinn, and his eyes were red rimmed as if he'd been crying. "Dinner?"

Swallowing her own tears, she nodded before drawing both her guys into a hug.

"I CAN'T TELL you how excited I am to finally meet you."

"I feel the same," Pandora said. Calder's mother's sincerity showed in the strength of her hug. She'd gotten to the steak house ahead of Pandora and her son and grandson. "I'm sorry we weren't able to meet in North Carolina."

Calder's mother looked to her son and scowled. "Me, too."

Pandora held Quinn, who'd fallen asleep during the walk from the parking lot. She'd forgotten how good the simple act of holding him felt.

When Calder helped her ease into a booth, then slid in beside her, Pandora tried ignoring the warm tingles flooding through her from his lightest touch, but he was a hard man to ignore.

"Let me have him." Calder took his sleepy boy, settling him into his detachable car-seat carrier.

Calder's mom extended her hand across the table for Pandora to shake. "We've yet to be formally introduced. I'm Gloria."

"Pandora," she said with a laugh and easy smile. Something about the older woman put her instantly at ease. She had her son's eyes, only in a wiser, more at-peace version.

"My guess is Quinn's happy to see his favorite nanny." Gloria took a blanket from the diaper bag Calder had set next to his son's carrier, then draped it over the sleeping infant. "This is the first time I've seen him truly rest since I've been with him."

"I missed him, too." And his dad. But no way was Pandora admitting that.

The waitress came and went.

Small talk ebbed and flowed.

Only after dessert and coffee had been served did Gloria raise the evening's stakes. While stirring cream into her coffee, she said, "I'm leaving first thing in the morning. Calder, since tomorrow's Friday and you're due back on base Monday, what are your plans for your son?"

"I'd hoped to have Pandora back home, but…" As his words trailed off, he ran his left pinkie along hers—just barely. It wouldn't be noticeable to anyone but her. Pandora felt it low in her belly. Somersaults of pure heat rushed through her, robbing her of all rational thought. "She kinda turned me down."

"Can't say as I blame her." Pandora was touched by Gloria's understanding her point of view. "Only, as we discussed, my reasons are different from hers." Turning to Pandora, she said, "For a moment, though, please humor me by considering an alternate offer from what Calder had in mind."

"O-okay…." Pandora wasn't sure what to think, but out of respect for her new friend, she'd be receptive to whatever Gloria proposed.

Hands clasped in front of her on the table, Gloria took a deep breath, slowly exhaled then smiled. "Here's what I'm thinking. Pandora, the nature of Calder's job means he has to have someone reliable in Quinn's life. That said, as long as he's in town, would you be amenable to watching Quinn solely during the day?"

"How much has your son told you about my past?"

"Everything."

Lips pressed, Pandora nodded. Might as well lay it all on the table. "My last chance to regain legal custody of my daughter will be at a March court hearing. In preparation for that, I follow a strict set of guidelines that have been set for me by my Social Services caseworker." Mouth dry, she sipped ice water. "Those guidelines include maintaining a permanent residence that will be suitable for my child, as well as keeping full-time employment."

Calder asked, "Can't you get both of those things with me?"

"Not on my terms." Pandora would've preferred speaking with Calder about the issue in private, but now that it was out there, she wouldn't back down. "As much as I've grown to love Quinn, my daughter is my primary goal. To get her back full-time, I have to be better than perfect—one hundred percent of the time. Until my hearing, I cannot—*will not* move from my current address. In the same respect, I can't take the risk of you discovering something about me you don't like and once again letting me go."

"Don't pull that." He raised his palms as if intent on slamming them against the table, but then thought better of it and calmed himself before losing control. "Had you told me everything you went through right from the start, this whole thing might have played out differently."

"Get over it. You can't deny I ever gave Quinn anything but expert care. As for my private life—it's *private*. The only reason I told you anything was because you made me feel as if I could trust you. Now I know those instincts were wrong. At this point, I can't take any more chances on you, Calder—at least not before my custody hearing."

Gloria appeared crestfallen. "Please, Pandora…"

"I said I wouldn't take a chance on your son, but for your

grandson?" She couldn't help but smile. "I can't get enough of him. I want to be there when he takes his first steps and says his first real words. What I propose is that Calder drop him off at the day care where I work each morning on his way to the base. I'll personally care for Quinn, and honestly, I think he'd enjoy socializing with the other kids." Hoping what she next proposed never came to pass, she said to Calder, "If you're deployed before you find a suitable full-time nanny, I would be honored if you'd allow Quinn to stay with me, in my home, where I promise he'll get the love and attention I wish I could give my own child."

Wiping tears from her cheeks, Gloria said, "I don't know about you, Calder, but that sounds like an ideal compromise to me."

He nodded. "Thank you. I think that'll work fine."

After paying the bill, Gloria left for the restroom.

On their own, Calder fixed her with a stare of such intensity she felt as if he'd kissed her all over again, and just like the last time, her traitorous body liked it. "For the record, I'm hereby issuing you a promise that I'll never again let you down."

I want to believe you, her emotional side wanted to say, but the more rational part of her said, "I wish I could believe you."

"THAT WENT WELL," Gloria said from the sofa when he walked in the door with Quinn after taking Pandora home. "She's a lovely girl. I see why you like her."

He took Quinn from his carrier, holding him on his lap when he all but collapsed into the armchair. Damn, all this emotional stuff was tiring.

Having slept through dinner, Quinn was now wired. He squirmed until Calder set him on the carpet where he crawled to the coffee table and tugged himself up, giggling and shrieking the whole way.

"Glad you had fun." He kicked off his Sperrys, then landed his feet atop the same table. "Personally, I thought it was a train wreck."

"Because you had to compromise?" Gloria sipped wine from a juice glass.

"I apologized. Repeatedly. There's not much else I can do." The whole thing had exhausted him. He was seriously ready for bed, but with Quinn wide-awake and still needing his bath, Calder didn't see sleep in his near future.

"Know what else you can do?" his mom asked. "Instead of just telling Pandora you're sorry. *Show* her."

"How?"

She tickled Quinn's belly. "That's something only you can decide."

AFTER ENTERING HER apartment, Pandora closed and locked the door, then leaned against it

What a night—in many ways.

She couldn't even begin processing the multitude of conflicting dynamics. Part of her had been downright giddy over once again holding Quinn in her arms. Meeting Gloria had been a joy, especially since her own mother was long since gone. But then there'd been Calder.

At times he'd been almost flirty, others defensive, others still powerfully persuasive.

It would've been so easy giving in to him, and she'd appreciated his apologies, but she wasn't ready for *more*.

Would she ever be? Who knew?

Right now, her sole focus had to be Julia.

"DID YOU AT LEAST like his mom?" Natalie asked at the first yard sale of their Saturday morning. Pandora had already given her a play-by-play of how the evening had broken down—skipping the part about Calder's unfair tactics with his pinkie finger.

"A lot. Oh—and you should be hearing from Calder about him enrolling Quinn in the infant class."

"Nope." She flipped through a stack of CDs. "After what he did to you, I blackballed him."

"I appreciate your mama lion instincts, but I'll be the first to admit my past isn't exactly popular résumé material. A part of me can't fault Calder for being concerned as to who's caring for his son. And why should Quinn be penalized? He deserves the best care."

"You raise interesting points." Holding out a CD, she asked, "What're your thoughts on *A Dean Martin Christmas?*"

"Never too early to bring a touch of class to your holiday playlist."

"Exactly."

By lunchtime, Pandora had found two poppy-colored throw pillows for the living room couch, a fairly decent oil painting of a sunset she thought would look great over the mantel, more books and a gorgeous set of dishes. She'd even picked up an older-model TV for fifteen bucks.

Pandora said her goodbyes to Natalie, then returned home to arrange her purchases. After a shower, she fixed her hair in preparation for her three-o'clock visit with Julia. Their meeting time was later than usual, but she wasn't complaining.

She'd just finished blow-drying her hair when a knock sounded on the door. She drew back the curtain to find Calder holding Quinn.

The moment the infant caught sight of her, he bucked and kicked, struggling to reach her.

She opened the door, took the baby then shot Calder a dirty look. "May I help you?"

"Sure hope so." He held up a bag of groceries, then brushed past her as if he was a man on a mission. "Mom ended up not catching a flight till this morning, and since Quinn's been mopey, I thought you might want to help cheer him up."

"Where are you going?" She closed the door.

"To your kitchen. While you're playing with the baby, I'm making my world-famous spaghetti."

Hands on her hips, she cocked her head. "I wasn't aware you know how to cook anything."

"I don't." His wink and sexy slow grin had her regretting her earlier decision to steer clear of him. "Mom gave me her recipe. Can't be too hard, right?"

She couldn't keep from grinning herself. "While that sounds great—especially the part about me cheering this little darling—" she kissed the top of Quinn's head "—I'm meeting my daughter in just under two hours. I usually leave an hour early, though. If a wreck or traffic caused me to be late, that could potentially hurt my case."

"Can I go?" He brushed past her, setting the groceries on the kitchen table. "I'd love to meet your Julia."

"No." She sat on the hearth, setting Quinn on the floor in front of her, holding his hands to help him walk.

"That was fast."

"Sorry, but Julia's visits are sacred. I would never introduce a man to her unless we were in a committed relationship—even then, if she so much as utters one syllable about not liking him, he's out."

"Knowing kids, isn't that unrealistic?" He unpacked the food.

"After what my ex put her through—no. For a while, she was afraid of all men. Counseling has finally helped. And why are you putting Parmesan cheese in my fridge? I don't have time for you to cook anything."

"I was thinking while you have a nice visit with Julia, Quinn and I will hang back here making you a meal. You have to eat, right?"

Sure, but being around him set her so on edge, she'd lost her appetite. No matter how much she denied it, she was still hopelessly attracted to the man—she craved another kiss like Santa craves cookies. "All right, you can stay, but first you have to tell me your endgame."

"What do you mean?" He'd set Italian sausage on the counter, using a steak knife to slit open the package.

"When you asked me to leave, you made it clear you wanted nothing to do with me and now you're cooking dinner? I'm a recovering alcoholic. I served time—not much, but more than enough to know I'm never going back to that place. Worst crime of all? My child was legally removed from my home."

"Knowing all that, then seeing the woman you are today?" He shook his head. "Hell, I admire you. Sure, I still have a lot of questions, but mostly I just kick myself for letting you get away."

While waiting in the Social Services lobby, Pandora couldn't get Calder's words from her head. Was he sincere? Or was he panicked over not having her around to help watch Quinn? He'd mentioned still having questions. Once he learned her ex could one day be eligible for parole and occasionally sent letters begging to see Julia, would Calder want nothing to do with her all over again?

She might have a squeaky-clean new life on the outside, but on the inside, even she knew she had miles to go before being fully healed. For that matter, did anyone ever fully heal from an addiction?

With still twenty minutes to go, she folded her arms and paced. She was always excited to see her little girl, but even more so today. She couldn't wait to tell Julia about her bedroom. The way sunshine would be her new alarm clock.

Calder? Where does he fit in? And Quinn?

Hands to her temples, she almost wished Calder had never entered her life. He'd made her yearn for the kind of Ward and June Cleaver normalcy she'd only dreamed existed. It wasn't practical for her to believe magic could strike twice.

"Mommy!" Julia entered the building with her foster parents, but from her first sight of Pandora, she released Cindy's hand and made a beeline for her.

Heart swelling with happiness, Pandora crushed her daughter in a hug. "You smell good. Like sugar cookies. Been baking?"

"Uh-huh!" She looked to her foster mother. "Mom Cindy got new cookie cutters and we practiced for Thanksgiving. I made a turkey!"

"That's awesome!" Pandora rewarded her clever girl with another hug.

"Ready?" asked the social worker who supervised Pandora's visits.

"Where's Quinn?" Julia asked when they settled at a table to color the new princess coloring book Pandora had brought her.

"He's with his dad today."

"Is he nice?"

"Quinn's dad?"

"Uh-huh…." Julia concentrated so hard on staying inside the lines that she'd drawn her lower lip into her mouth.

"He's very nice."

"My dad scared me. He was mean to you."

Where had that come from? "Yes, sweetie, he was. I'm sorry."

"Mom Cindy's husband is real nice. He fixed my bike tire and learned me how to climb trees."

"You mean he taught you?" she corrected, smoothing Julia's ponytail.

"Yeah. It was fun. I didn't know dads could be fun. I thought they were all scary."

A too-familiar knot formed at the back of Pandora's throat. Honestly, until meeting Calder, she hadn't known, either. But she was learning....

"Done!" She held up her completed princess picture.

"It's beautiful," Pandora said. "Could I please keep it to put on my new fridge?"

"Only if I get to keep yours to put on *my* fridge!" Julia hopped and clapped after her request, reminding Pandora of the lighthearted banter they'd occasionally shared when she'd been very young.

"That's a deal."

As usual, two hours passed way too fast, but when the social worker asked Pandora if she'd like a special Christmas visit, Pandora felt she was definitely on track for winning her March case.

"Dude, seriously?" Calder was already having enough trouble following his mom's recipe. Not only couldn't he read her handwriting, but he'd bought the wrong tomato stuff. Who knew there was a difference between paste and stewed and just plain old sauce? It all looked the same to him. Now Quinn had helped himself to Pandora's lower cabinets, tugging out all the pots and pans, laughing and squealing with each clang. "Sorry, but this isn't going to work."

Calder made a makeshift baby corral from the sofa cushions and coffee table, then set Quinn in the middle with a few toys from his diaper bag.

He'd barely made it back to the kitchen before his son let loose with a wail that sounded as if he'd been stabbed.

Calder ran back in, picked up his bawling son. "Don't you want me to impress Pandora with this fancy dinner?"

Quinn answered with more ear-piercing screams.

What to do? What to do?

The usual panic set in when Calder couldn't calm his son. He was hardly ever fussy with Pandora, but he had been with Gloria. What had Pandora done to appease him?

Remembering her pacing and singing with the occasional rocking motion thrown in, Calder tried cradling Quinn close to his chest.

"I'm not Sinatra," Calder said, "but here goes…"

As best as he could, fudging at least half the words, Calder sang and rocked his son.

PANDORA TRIED SQUELCHING the seed of excitement growing inside her when she saw Calder's car still in her driveway.

With Julia's picture and her purse in hand, she locked up her car and climbed the stairs leading to her apartment. At the top, instead of slipping her key in the lock, she stopped to listen.

Was Calder singing?

Peeking through a part in the curtains, she found him not only crooning to his son, but on his knees, holding Quinn's hands, dancing with him. The best part was that Calder wasn't even going with a nursery rhyme, but vintage Journey.

Judging by the smile on Quinn's face, he loved it.

She soundlessly opened the door, wanting to view more of the adorable scene, but Quinn caught sight of her and dropped to his knees, crawling her way. "Hey, cutie!"

Grabbing onto her slacks, he raised himself upright, pinching for her to lift him.

"How'd it go?" Calder asked. Was it her imagination or was his face a shade redder from getting caught being a not-so-manly SEAL? What he didn't know was that she found this softer side infinitely more attractive—not a good thing, considering her intent to remain man-free.

Chapter Fourteen

Fanning herself from the heat just looking at Calder raised in her cheeks, Pandora asked, "Do you have the oven on?"

"No. Why?"

"I'm warm." She removed the hat and gloves the blustery day's temperature had called for, set them on the nearby kitchen table then picked up Quinn. "Did you have fun exploring?"

"Gaa! Baa!"

"Well, that sounds interesting," she teased.

"How was your daughter?" Calder asked.

"Wonderful." She tilted her head back and closed her eyes, remembering her little girl's smile. "I know that old saying about not wishing your life away, but in this case, I'd give anything for it to already be March."

"Is your hearing early March or late?" He picked up sofa cushions from the floor.

"Early. What happened?" She nodded toward her pillaged couch.

"Thought I might outsmart my Tasmanian devil by corralling him, but turns out he's way smarter than me."

"I know the feeling." She kissed the infant's nose. "So where's this fabulous meal you promised? I'm starving." Walking the ten feet to the kitchen, she explored the stove and oven.

"Um, yeah… Have you ever tried cooking while a Tasmanian devil circles your feet?"

"As a matter of fact, I have. Welcome to my world."

They shared a laugh, which surprised Pandora. When Calder sent her away, she'd honestly feared never laughing again.

Neither of them had the energy to figure out where Calder's sauce had gone wrong, so he ordered a pizza and Pandora scrambled an egg for Quinn to go along with his bottle.

After eating, the baby drifted off to sleep, leaving Pandora achingly aware that she and Calder were alone. The sensation reminded her of their nights back at his house. How sometimes they'd watch a movie or just hang out in the living room reading. What they hadn't done was spend a lot of time talking—no doubt largely because of her unwillingness to open up about her past.

"Here we are again." Calder shot a slow grin her way. "Seems like we always end up just sitting."

"Sure sign of parental exhaustion—not that I'm Quinn's parent, but you know what I mean."

"Yeah." After a few more seconds' silence during which she wasn't sure what to do with her hands, he asked, "If it's not too personal, tell me about your ex."

"Wow…" She shook her head. "Talk about jumping straight from the shallow to the deep end."

"You don't have to answer. Guess I feel like I know you better than anyone else, yet when I really think about it, I hardly know anything about you."

"Feeling's mutual." She reached across the sofa to jab his shoulder. He was all muscle to the point his skin hardly had any give. Eyes briefly closed, she struggled to forget the sight of him doing a towel-wrapped shower dash to his room. His bare chest still glistening from the water.

"All right, ask me anything. I'm an open book."

Where did she start? Careful to avoid any more thoughts of his pecs—not to mention those six-pack abs—she asked, "Why is a guy like you still single?"

"I assume you mean such a handsome man?" There he went again with the grin that never failed to stir needs she'd believed long gone.

"Among other things." Squelching the familiar urge to fan herself, she said, "I'm serious. You've got a great job. You seem reasonably smart—except when it comes to caring for small children...." She winked.

Now he was jabbing her. "Watch it. I resent that statement." He rubbed the back of his neck, then groaned. "Where do I even start? When I was in North Carolina, I had a great talk with my stepdad. Mom, too, but it was Harold who unwittingly lit a lightbulb in my head."

"Oh?" Intrigued, she kicked off her loafers to sit with her legs tucked beneath her, angling to face him.

"My folks split when I was eight. Dad cheated, but oddly enough, there wasn't much fighting. I think I was more upset than my mom. He moved to Nebraska and on school breaks I was required to stay with him. Seems like every time I went, he had a different wife who made a big deal out of being my stepmom. By the time I was in high school, it was ridiculous." He shrugged. "I didn't understand the point of marrying someone—or even being in a relationship with her—if it would only end badly. Easier to avoid the issue altogether, you know?"

"Interesting...." She couldn't help but draw comparisons to their lives. "Even though I watched my mom live in a horrible marriage, after she died, I wanted my own marriage so badly that right after high school I ran off to get married—to a man who treated me worse than my father. You, on the other hand, did the opposite of what you'd seen as a child.

Maybe a few years from now I'd like to take a few online college psychology courses."

"You'd probably be good at psychology. Since you've experienced so much, I think you'd be able to help a lot of people."

"Really?" No one had ever said something like that to her before—that she might be good at something. Oh, sure, Natalie told her all the time she was good with kids, but this was different. Her interactions with children felt more like play than a job.

"Of course." He edged sideways to better face her. "I wouldn't say it if I didn't mean it. Now that I realize you're the real deal—you actually beat the kinds of addictions that haunt people their entire lives—even kill them—I'm impressed."

"Thank you." Fairly glowing from his kind words, she found herself not wanting the night to end. How differently would things be between them now if she'd been open with Calder from the start? Would they be holding hands? Kissing? *More?*

She snatched a magazine from an end table, back to fanning flaming cheeks.

"You okay?" he asked.

"Really good."

"Me, too."

He smiled.

She smiled. "There's a swap meet at the fairgrounds tomorrow. I thought I might go. Pick up a few things for the apartment. Think you and Quinn would want to tag along?"

"Sure. What time?"

"It starts at ten. Is that all right?" Her heart galloped while awaiting his reply. Would she ever feel normal around him? Did she even want to?

"Perfect. Quinn and I will pick you up. In the meantime…" He looked to his son. "Guess I'd better get this guy to bed."

After helping Calder gather Quinn's baby gear, she walked him to the door.

For the longest time Calder just stood there with his hand on the knob. He acted apprehensive, as if he wanted to say something but couldn't quite make the words come. "Well…"

She flashed a nervous smile, willing her runaway pulse to slow. Why, when he'd hurt her so badly, would she have given anything right now for him to kiss her?

"Guess I'll see you in the morning." He tried hugging her, but with Quinn's carrier bumping their knees, much to Pandora's everlasting regret any closeness proved impossible.

A good thing? Pandora honestly didn't know.

"Again?" Quinn had slept the entire ride home, only to now be wired. "I've got to get you on a schedule, bud."

"Gaaaaah!"

"My thoughts exactly."

Calder bathed his son, having a little too much fun with Quinn's impressive boat collection. After drying him, just as he'd seen Pandora and his mother do, he rubbed lotion on Quinn's bottom, then diapered him, concentrating extra hard on keeping the adhesive tabs even.

"Hungry?" he asked.

"Goooooo bah!"

"Dad-dee."

"Gaaaaaah bah!"

"Dad-dee."

Instead of speaking, the kid blew a raspberry containing enough drool to send them back to the bathroom for a fresh face wash.

For the life of him, Calder couldn't remember if Pandora and his mom fed Quinn right before bed or not. Personally,

Calder was always sleepy after a big meal, but maybe that wasn't the case with kids.

How was it possible that he'd had Quinn since summer and he still didn't have his schedule nailed down? Was that what his mom meant about forcing him to get to know his son?

"How about we both get a snack?"

In the kitchen, he foraged. He found plenty for himself, but he wasn't sure about feeding a protein bar to a baby.

"I'll sure be glad when you can just say what you want."

"Bah!"

"You want a bottle?"

"Dah!"

"Dad-dee?"

"Goooo dah!"

"You do know you're making me feel crazy?"

Quinn grabbed his father's nose and squeezed.

Calder was exhausted, but considering a certain hyper infant showed no sign of sleeping any time soon, Calder popped the original *Total Recall* in the DVD player, settling in for a long night.

"What do you think Pandora's doing?"

"Paaaah?"

"Pan-dor-a."

"Pah hor!"

"Pan-door-rah."

Though his favorite movie played on TV, it'd become much more entertaining trying to get Quinn to say Pandora's name.

WHEN CALDER YAWNED for the tenth time in five minutes as they strolled the bustling flea market and Quinn slept soundly in his stroller, Pandora asked, "What'd you two do last night after you left?"

"I wanted to go to bed, but Mr. Party Animal refused."

"I had him on a great schedule. What happened?" The moment she asked the question, Pandora regretted it. What had happened was Calder sent her on her way. Despite bright sun and the party atmosphere provided by a local swing band, her mood plummeted.

"We both know I screwed up." He sidestepped three boys wielding squirt guns. "You don't have to rub my nose it."

"That wasn't my intent—even though that is what happened. And for the record—" she veered the stroller toward a towering oak, its shade protecting a picnic table "—I understand why you sent me away. If our roles had been reversed and I'd hired you to watch Julia, I'd have done the same. Bringing up the schedule was an honest mistake. I didn't mean anything by it."

He'd shoved his hands into his jeans pockets. "While we're talking about issues probably better left alone…" He sighed and picked at the bark on a nearby oak. "In retrospect, I'm not entirely sure my reaction was all about you. Your past."

"What do you mean?" She brushed crumbs from the table's bench, then had a seat.

"I don't even know how to say this." He looked to the cloudless blue sky, then to her.

"Good grief, Calder, whatever it is, spit it out. Lord knows I've spilled enough of my dirty secrets."

"Looking back on it, your news relieved me. What I felt for you—" he sat beside her, easing his fingers between hers "—it happened too fast. My whole life I shied away from anything real, yet there you were. You scared me. My own feelings scared me."

He straddled the bench, cupping his hand to her face, brushing her cheek with his thumb. Though the crowded sale went on around them, Pandora felt sheltered on an island created by Calder's confession. He cared about her.

"Hell…" He chuckled, leaning close enough to send her

pulse deep into the danger zone. "I'm scared right now, but apparently not smart enough to run."

"Maybe it's time to stop running?"

He kissed her deliciously slow and sweet. He kissed her until she was tilting her head to allow him deeper access and closing her eyes with a sigh.

"Pandora? Is that you and little Quinn?"

Still in a kiss-induced fog, Pandora glanced up to see Lila with her husband in tow.

"I told her to leave you two alone," Martin grumbled.

"Oh, hush." Lila gave her husband a swat. "I haven't seen you in forever, and you missed last week's beautification meeting."

As high as Pandora had been moments earlier, she was now that low. What did she say? Lila knew nothing about her past.

Calder settled his arm around her shoulders. "Quinn and I are so proud of her. She landed a great new job at the day care her agency runs. Quinn starts there Monday."

"How exciting." Lila gave her a quick hug. "But does this mean you're no longer living in the neighborhood?"

"No," Calder again answered for her, "but, hopefully, she'll be over for lots of visits."

Lila hugged her again, and after more small talk, the elderly couple ambled on.

"Thanks," Pandora said to Calder. "I didn't know what to say."

"Like you once told me, there's really nothing to say. The past is past." He kissed the tip of her nose. "Let's keep it that way."

THE NIGHT BEFORE Thanksgiving, Calder coached his son during bath time. "Pan-dor-a."

"Paa gah!"

"Pan-door-rah."

"Ah gah roo!" Splash, splash.

Calder rocked back on his heels. "Dude, you're killing me. Do you know how much it would mean to Pandora if you said her name?"

"Goo goo goo!" Quinn was too busy with his boats to pay any more attention, and to be truthful, this had also become Calder's favorite part of the day. Though he now *played* with boats of a much larger scale, he'd forgotten how much fun small boats could be.

As frustrated as he'd been with his mom for abandoning him to care for Quinn on his own, Calder was now thankful. He'd mastered almost every aspect of infant care, though he still struggled with the tiny snaps now and then.

He gave Quinn a good scrub, then readied him for bed.

Back on the schedule Pandora had written for him, Quinn now had a small bottle before bed, then Calder cleaned his son's teeth before settling him into his crib.

While Calder liked the feeling of accomplishment caring for his son all on his own gave him, he also sorely missed Pandora being with him in the evenings after Quinn drifted off to sleep.

Never in a million years would he have thought he'd envy his friends Deacon and Garrett, but he found himself wanting to share his time with Quinn with Pandora—not because he expected her to perform any of the work, but because he missed sharing small milestones he knew she'd enjoy.

One day soon, Quinn would say his first word, take his first solo steps. Calder wanted Pandora to be there, sharing each and every one of those special moments.

What about her daughter?

The thought hadn't escaped him that Pandora and Julia were a package deal. It'd taken months for him to adjust to being a father to his own child. How would he cope with parenting another man's daughter? One who no doubt carried a staggering amount of emotional baggage?

On autopilot, he reached for a beer, but then put it back in the fridge. He didn't need liquor to deal with this issue; he needed to open his heart. Julia was the same age he'd been when Harold had become a true father to him. Was it time for Calder to pay forward the favor?

If so, how would he know?

Chapter Fifteen

The only way Pandora could be happier would be if Julia had shared this beautiful day with her and all her friends. With a fire crackling in the fireplace, the traditional Thanksgiving meal devoured and her small kitchen cleaned, her apartment's living room had been transformed into a casino. The makeshift dining table they'd assembled from plywood and sawhorses with everyone bringing their own folding chairs was now the scene of a poker tournie using candy corn for chips. So far, Martin was beating the pants off everyone.

Holding Quinn, Pandora watched Cooper and Mason go all in while Heath and Patricia folded. Natalie and Anna conferred on what to do with their poker hands.

Calder spied them. "Hey! No fair playing in teams."

Lila sipped her wine. "What does it hurt? You guys are trouncing the ladies."

The game continued with plenty more good-natured ribbing.

A year earlier, Pandora wouldn't have believed it possible for her life to now be so full. Yet here she sat, surrounded by friends who felt more like family than her real family ever had.

Turning in his chair, Calder said, "How about letting me hold Quinn and you get in on the next game?"

"Thanks, but I'm right where I want to be."

The night wound on, with Martin claiming bragging rights until Lila informed him it was time to go.

The remaining guys disassembled the big table, moving their game to the kitchen table while the women got a jump start on the next holiday by watching *Christmas Vacation,* which Pandora had picked up at a thrift store, along with a secondhand DVD player.

Pandora shared the sofa with Natalie. Quinn lounged between them, plinking on his toy piano. Patricia and Anna sat in armchairs closer to the TV.

"How's it going between you and Calder?" Natalie asked in a conspiratorial tone.

"We're friends."

Eyebrows raised, she asked, "*Just* friends?"

"We've kissed…." Boy, had they kissed. Home from the swap meet, things had grown heated, but that was it. She wasn't sure she was ready for *more,* and being a gentleman, Calder had agreed to take things slow.

"I'm glad things are working out." Natalie jiggled Quinn's hippo rattle. "In my professional opinion, you two would be good for each other."

"Your *professional* opinion?" Grinning, now Pandora was the one raising her brows.

"Now that you've worked out your kinks, the three of you make a nice family. When Julia comes home, I'm sure she'll like him, too."

"Hope so." Pandora looked in Calder's direction. His dark hair had grown long, but she liked it. When he kissed her, she weaved her fingers through it, pressing him closer.

"He's gotten a lot better with Quinn, too. I haven't seen you attending to a single diaper all day."

"I know. He's a changed man."

"Just like you're a changed woman." Natalie took Pandora's hand, giving her a squeeze. "See what I mean? Match made in heaven."

"I want to believe that, but I'm afraid."

"What else could go wrong? He knows more about you than I do. Once Julia moves in here and she gets to know him, I predict wedding bells by next summer."

"Stop." She cast her friend a warning look.

"I'm just sayin'…"

"Yeah, well, quit sayin'. I got my hopes up once, and you saw where that led. For now, I'm taking life day by day."

Mason startled Pandora by shouting, "You're such a cheat, Hopper! No way did you just get dealt a royal flush."

"The hell I didn't!"

"Hey, whoa…" Calder broke them up. "Keep it down, I've got a kid over there." A kid who, thankfully, hadn't been spooked by his friend's outburst.

Cooper sighed. "I miss the good old days when it was just us guys playing for cash."

Heath dealt new hands. "You're just jealous you don't have a good woman. Me and Calder got it all figured out."

"You and the nanny are back in business?" Mason asked.

"Think so." Calder spread his cards. Nothing. Not even a lousy pair.

"Don't leave us hanging." Mason leaned in, making sure the women didn't overhear him. "So you're finally hooking up with the nanny?"

"Drop it," Calder said more harshly than he'd intended, but hopefully it got his point across. "She's way more than just Quinn's nanny."

"You're serious about her?" Heath asked. "If so, man, you need to elope. For me and Patricia, this whole wedding thing is out of control."

Calder slapped his cards to the table. "There's no wedding. We're just friends."

"With benefits?" Mason might be one of his best friends, but at the moment, Calder was on the verge of calling him outside for a *talk*.

"She's a good woman. My kid loves her. End of story." As to how Calder felt about her, all he knew was that even the simple act of staring across the room at her made his chest swell with anticipation for when they were finally alone.

"What a great day." Pandora plucked a few stray candy corns from the kitchen floor. "Hope everyone had as nice a time as I did."

Quinn had conked out in his carrier.

"Pretty sure fun was had by all except Mason, who'd better be glad we weren't playing for real money."

She smiled. Bone-deep contentment didn't come close to describing the way her body hummed when Calder drew her into his arms.

"While we were playing, the guys raised a few legitimate questions."

"Oh?" she said against the warm wall of his chest.

"Mason asked if we're an item. I didn't know what to tell him. I mean, we've never really talked about any of this."

"Define *this*..." She skimmed her free hand along his ridiculously chiseled abs. What would they feel like without his shirt?

"Where do I begin? I wouldn't know how to define it. Are we going steady? That sounds so fifties-era high school. Are you my girlfriend? See what I mean? Do we even need a definition? Can't we just have an understanding?"

"I suppose, but then you'd have to define that. What are your terms?" she asked.

"For starters—" he kissed the crown of her head "—I don't want any other guys within fifty feet of you."

"That might be tough," she teased, "considering my favorite student happens to be your son."

"You know what I mean. I want you strictly for myself."

"That's all good and well, but what happens when you find a sitter and decide you need a night of barhopping? What if I have a problem sharing you?"

He tipped her head back, kissing her slow and breathless and dizzy. "I suppose a mutually beneficial agreement could be arranged. Any further demands?"

"More of this…." To make sure he got the message, this time she was the one kissing him, only the day's heady pleasure left her hungry for more than the leftovers stocking the fridge. Emboldened by happiness, she slid her hands under his shirt, finally sampling those abs she'd been dreaming of. His warm, sinewy strength didn't disappoint.

He groaned. "What're you doing to me?"

"What we've both been craving…."

Braver still, she undid the button on his jeans, then lowered the zipper. He'd gone commando and her actions set him free.

Giggling, she said, "Oops."

"Now, that's embarrassing." There was no doubt about him being on board with whatever came next—assuming that meant a long-awaited trip to her bedroom.

"It shouldn't be." Caressing the swollen length of him, she knelt to give him further pleasure, but he stopped her, drawing her up. "What's wrong?"

With a hand on her chin, he forced her gaze to his. "Are you sure this is what you want?"

Nodding, she smiled. "All I really know is I want—need—this closeness. I've lost so much in my life. I can't lose you."

"I'm not going anywhere." He kissed her forehead and cheeks and nose and finally, finally, her lips before taking her hand. "Come on. The kiddo's down for the count. Let's take full advantage of that situation." Taking her hand, he guided her to her room.

Once there, she began unbuttoning his shirt, but he again halted her progress. "The second part of the speech I started a minute ago was that this first time is especially for you." He kissed her soft and slow and thoroughly, all the while tugging up her sweater, pausing only long enough to drag it over her head. He tossed the garment to the floor and lowered his lips to her throat and collarbone and the tops of her breasts before also removing her bra.

The heat from the fire hadn't made it to her room. The sudden chill hardened her nipples, but he soon had her warm by rubbing his palm over one and suckling the other.

By the time he'd lowered his seeking mouth to her abdomen, then lower still to unhook her skirt's waistband and let it pool with a whisper around her feet, her breathing had become ragged.

He removed her leather pumps, rolled down her navy tights. When all that remained of her clothing were the lacy scrap of her panties, he opened his mouth against her sensitive mound, exhaling tantalizingly warm air against her most private area. He made her shiver, but not because she was cold.

Hands pressed to the back of his head, she spread her legs, inviting him—needing him—to explore farther. He dragged down her panties before backing her against the bed. Pushing her back until her calves dangled against the edge of the bed, he lowered his mouth again, this time trailing a line of shiver-inducing kisses from her ankle to the growing hum between her legs.

By the time he kissed more, then inserted one finger and then two, she could scarcely control her fevered emotions. She bucked against him, all at once needing release, yet never wanting the building, budding waves of pure sensation to stop.

"I—I need you inside me," she barely found breath to say.

"Shh…" Ignoring her, he performed more wicked tricks with his tongue before sensations transformed to even more paralyzing pressure. Thrashing her head to and fro, she thrust her fingers into his hair. Higher and higher waves of pure pleasure carried her until she could no longer think and barely even breathe. When release finally came, it manifested in a white-hot explosion behind her closed eyes.

Shivering, sweating, exhausted yet eager for more, she drew him up, begging him for additional sweet release.

He fished a condom from his jeans pocket, then whole-heartedly obliged.

THE WEDNESDAY AFTER Thanksgiving, Pandora had just disinfected the last of the three-year-old classroom toys when she saw Calder headed her way. He hadn't yet grabbed Quinn from the infants' room, and her kids were all gone for the day. Was it wrong to be so excited for their few minutes alone?

"On my lunch break," she said, pressing her hands to his chest before sneaking in a kiss, "I found the cutest decoration idea for a boy's room. My visitation with Julia is early on Saturday, so after that, do you want to see if we can tackle building a battleship bookcase in Quinn's room?"

"I would love to, but I've got bad news."

Nerves seized her system. What else could he possibly have learned about her to turn him against her? "I've told you *everything*…."

"Baby, no…" Framing her face with his hands, he pressed his lips to hers with an urgency he hadn't before shown. "You're all I've ever wanted. I'm shipping out in the morning."

She'd expected his news to concern her—not him. Now that she knew the truth, she'd have almost rather it had concerned her. At least that way he wouldn't be in danger.

"I want to spend the rest of my time here with you and Quinn. Stay the night with me?"

Unable to speak past the fear knotting her throat, she nodded.

"This is nice." The November night was calm and not too chilly. By the light of a nearly full moon, they'd packed a picnic and headed for a deserted beach, where Calder built a small fire for hot dogs and marshmallows.

Calder held Quinn a safe distance from the fire, helping him hold his marshmallow stick. "Okay, bud, the secret to a great marshmallow is catching it on fire, then sucking out the gooey insides."

"You can't let him eat that charred stuff," Pandora protested.

"I've eaten it all my life and look how big and strong I am. You want him to be a man, don't you?"

"Well, sure, but not if it means his poor belly's going to be filled with charcoal."

"Hear that, buddy? Your mom thinks we don't know what we're doing." He pulled the flaming ball from the fire and blew it out, waiting for it to cool a few seconds before eating the crispy outer layer, then letting Quinn lick the gooey part.

"Calder?"

"Hmm?"

"Did you mean to say what you just did?" She loaded her own marshmallow onto a stick, poking it into the fire.

"What?"

"You referred to me as Quinn's mom. Is that how you really feel?"

He met her gaze to find her sincere, which left him wondering about his own intentions. Honestly, the slip had been unconscious. Above all, he wanted to keep the mood light. Mellow. He didn't want to cover anything heavy. He needed this mental image to keep with him during the endless black nights ahead. He needed to know normalcy waited for him as soon as he got home.

"Calder?"

"Yeah?" He shrugged. "Sure. I guess that's how I feel. Think about it. Since Quinn's arrival, you're the only mom he's known. It makes sense."

"It also implies we're a heckuva lot more involved than simple boyfriend and girlfriend."

"That what you want?" He dug through the diaper bag for the wipes to clean Quinn's sticky face and hands. "To make things official?"

"You mean get married?" Her eyes widened.

"I suppose that's what people do. You don't have to look so shocked."

"I'm not. I guess I haven't really thought about it—wait, that's not true." As if dazed, she shook her head. "Of course I've thought about it, but in daydreams, you know? Guess I never believed someone like you would want someone like me."

"You know how crazy that sounds, don't you?" With one arm still holding Quinn a safe distance from the fire, he shifted her glasses on top of her head. "You're beautiful."

Ducking her head, she said, "Thanks, but we both know this goes deeper than looks. Calder, I have a child you've never even met. When Julia comes home, she'll have a lot of adjusting. What happens if you two don't get along?"

He snapped his stick in half, tossing it into the crackling fire. "Think I haven't thought of that?"

"I'm sorry. I know this isn't how you wanted our night to go."

"It's okay." He released Quinn just long enough to pick up the boy's hat from where the infant had tossed it a couple feet away.

"Calder, look…"

"I know we'll eventually hash this out, but can't it wait till I get home?"

"Um, this isn't about us, but your son. *Look.*"

Calder turned his attention to Quinn only to gasp. "I'll be damned…."

Quinn stood all on his own, pointing at the fire. *"Gah!"*

Arching his head back, Calder looked to the heavens. He'd never been much for church, but he had to believe someone was up there looking out for him tonight. If he'd missed his son's first solo steps, he'd have been devastated.

TOGETHER, PANDORA AND Calder bathed Quinn. While Calder fixed his son a bottle, Pandora dressed the boy in his fuzzy pj's. She'd missed this most special part of each day. To know she'd now get Quinn to herself each night was small consolation considering his father would be in danger.

Calder returned with Quinn's snack. "Mind if I feed him?"

"No. Of course not." She passed Quinn over to his dad and when Calder settled into the nursery rocker, cradling his son, Pandora struggled to control her runaway emotions. As Calder softly sang "Lullaby and Goodnight," she didn't even try hiding silent tears.

Calder had come such a long way as a parent since they'd first met. Quinn was a lucky boy.

Quinn fell asleep before finishing his bottle.

His father tucked him into his crib. When he turned away, it was to wipe his own tears.

In the hall, Calder said, "I never thought it was possible to hurt this bad. How do you stand being away from your daughter? Knowing she's so close yet untouchable."

"It's not easy. But I get by." She slipped her arms around his waist. "You will, too."

"My commanding officer warned this could be a long one. What if Quinn doesn't remember me by the time I get home?"

"If you'll record that beautiful song—" Pandora stood on tiptoe, pressing a simple yet heartfelt kiss to his lips "—I promise I'll make sure Quinn hears you every night."

"You'd do that for me?" he asked into her hair.

"Yes." *I'd do anything for you.*

"Ready to call it a night?" He held her and she nodded against him.

Taking her hand, he led her to the bed.

He faced her, settled his hands on her hips, nuzzling her neck until she feared her knees would buckle from desire. "You have no idea how much I want you."

"I—I feel the same." She unbuttoned her blouse, and this time he didn't try stopping her.

"I know this'll sound crazy, but I want—need—this to be different from other times. Slower, more deliberate. I need every detail burned to memory so I can call it up during especially dark nights."

"Of course," she whispered with a kiss.

Their lovemaking was as he'd requested—slow and beautiful and poignantly, painfully sweet.

After, they showered together, taking turns washing each other, ending up making love again beneath the hot spray.

Finally in bed, when Calder spooned her, and she knew their precious last few hours were ticking away, Pandora's heart shattered. "I don't want you to go," she said in a voice so quiet she wasn't sure she'd spoken at all.

"Likewise."

But when Pandora woke, Calder was gone.

Along with part of her heart.

DECEMBER WAS A BLUR.

Gloria and Harold, Calder's stepfather, had driven over

to spend time with Quinn. They were staying at Calder's house, and on Christmas they watched Quinn for Pandora so she could visit Julia.

The waiting area was surprisingly full. Carols played over the intercom and there was a table laden with cookies and punch. A new, softer side to Social Services? Pandora didn't mean to come across as bitter, but just as she was frightened for Calder, she was terrified something could go wrong at her hearing.

She was tired of this place. She'd done everything the judge and her caseworker had asked, and damn it, she wanted her child.

Julia bounded in, holding Mom Cindy's hand and wearing a red-velvet holiday dress with a black sash designed to look like Santa's belt. Everything about her was perfection, from her specially curled hair to her shiny new black-patent shoes. A pang ripped through Pandora. Even if she won her hearing, would she ever be able to provide a life as rich and full for her daughter as Mom Cindy and her doctor husband had?

While Julia excitedly rambled off the long list of toys Santa had brought, Pandora absorbed every word, wishing with all her heart she could scoop up her daughter and run. But where would she go? Calder and Quinn had also become her family. Only, with Calder now in Afghanistan and Julia still with her foster family, each day it became more of a struggle to get out of bed.

"Mommy?"

"Yes, sweetie?"

"Am I ever gonna live with you, or is Mom Cindy my mom now?" Her daughter's question not only caught her off guard but renewed her fighting spirit. Calder would eventually come home. So would her daughter.

"You know what court is, right?"

Julia nodded.

"In March, we go see a judge and he's going to let you come home with me. I have a nice new apartment and right now Quinn is even staying there until his dad comes home."

Julia brushed her new doll's blond hair. "Where's his dad?"

"A long way away. He's in the navy, and it's his job to protect us." Pandora refused to cry—not on what was supposed to be a happy day.

"Will I ever meet him?"

"I sure hope so. Right after you come home with me."

"Is he nice?"

Pandora's mind drifted to her heartbreakingly beautiful last night with Calder. "Yes, sweetie, he's a very nice man."

"Good." Her daughter snuggled against her. "I like Mom Cindy, but I love you. I miss you real bad."

"I miss you, too, pumpkin." She kissed the top of her curls. "Not much longer and I'll bring you home. We'll never be apart again."

"Promise, Mommy?"

Confident her third trip to court would be a charm, Pandora gave a playful tug on one of Julia's curls. "Promise."

Chapter Sixteen

After Christmas and New Year's and Quinn's sweet, simple January 3 first birthday celebrated at the day care with his grandparents and all his little friends, for Pandora each passing day, then week, that Calder still hadn't returned became studies in keeping herself busy. She'd bought a cheap digital camera and started scrapbooking her many photos of Quinn for Calder to have when he came home. She'd tried knitting but failed miserably. Baking was fun, but after an early February filled with heart-shaped cookies and cupcakes, Natalie gave her a well-meaning but firm lecture on the kids having had too many sweets.

Her hearing was scheduled for Friday, March 7 at the Norfolk Juvenile and Domestic Relations District Court.

She spent the days leading up to it working extra hard, trying to prevent having dreams or nightmares. The nightmares were always the same. She showed up in court and the judge found some excuse not to grant her custody. The dreams were even worse because she walked out of the courthouse into beautiful afternoon sun, holding hands with her little girl, only to wake in predawn darkness, realizing she hadn't truly been reunited with Julia. It had been a dream.

By the day of her hearing, Pandora was a mess. She hadn't slept, had no interest in eating and her stomach was knotted 24/7.

Natalie and Lila accompanied her.

Lila held her hand when they stepped into a courtroom crowded with other parents like Pandora. Somewhere in the large building, Julia and her Mom Cindy waited in a holding room. Was her daughter scared? Was she old enough to grasp the gravity of the day's importance?

Lila said, "Everything's going to be okay."

Incapable of speech, Pandora nodded.

It took ninety minutes before her case was called. She approached the judge's bench on legs so rubbery she was surprised she could even walk. Her heart adopted an unnaturally fast rhythm.

"Ms. Moore." The judge peered down at her from over his reading glasses. "First, let me commend you on not only making it to my court sober and in a timely manner, but for all the work you seem to have done to prove yourself a worthy mother. Your caseworker gave you rave reviews. I see a lot of cases run through here, and the way you've turned your life around is indeed impressive."

"Thank you, sir." Pandora had her hands so tightly clasped behind her that her nails dug into her sweating palms. She was afraid to hope his compliment meant her nightmare was nearly over.

"Actually, I'd like to thank you for being a shining example of how our system can work. You've followed everything on your case list to the letter—with the exception of housing. You were to have six months residing at the same address, but you only have four. Why is that?"

Pandora's mouth was so dry she feared not being able to speak. "Prior to that, sir, my job was as a live-in nanny, but my employer discovered my past and let me go."

"You mean you were fired?" The judge's bushy gray eyebrows shot up.

"Yes, sir, but not by the agency I work for. Just my boss.

Th-that's why I found a new home. But everything's fine now. He's currently deployed in Afghanistan, and I'm once again caring for his son."

Slapping her file on his bench, he removed his glasses, setting them atop her file. "Let me get this straight. This court removed a child from your custody, yet you're now caring for another child in an unsupervised manner?"

"Yes, sir, but I haven't had a drink in three years. I'm sorry for what happened last time I came before you. I really have turned my life around. Please, please give me back my child."

"Ms. Moore, I was fully prepared to return custody of your daughter. Now you've raised questions. Questions I believe at the very least merit further study of you and your perhaps too-lax caseworker before I can with clear conscience wholly declare you a fit mother. Your caseworker may be impressed by your improvements, but considering you've not fully met the requirements outlined on your case list…" Sighing, he turned to a woman seated at an adjoining lower desk. "Please schedule another hearing for Ms. Moore six months from now." He stared at Pandora. "Good day, Ms. Moore."

Pandora sat, stunned. Then she shouted, "Are you kidding me? I've done everything I possibly could to prove I'm a good mom. Yes, I made horrible mistakes, but I've paid for them over and over. Send my caseworker to my house to supervise me every day if that makes you feel better, but please, I'm begging you, don't make me wait another six months."

"Ms. Moore…" the judge warned.

"Please," Pandora begged, not bothering to hide her tears. Why was this happening? "You can't do this! I *promised!*"

The judge stood. "Do I need to call security?"

Pandora was barely conscious of Natalie and Lila charging up behind her, taking her by the arms and practically dragging her from the room.

"Got big plans for tonight?"

Late March, Calder looked up from the spy novel he'd only been skimming to find Mason grinning—never a good sign.

"If you don't, I was thinking we'd hit Tipsea's? Find a couple blondes? Or brunettes? Hell, doesn't much matter as long as they're wild and willing." He elbowed him from his seat in the noisy belly of their C-130.

"Sounds good, but I'll leave that to you and Cowboy. I want to surprise Pandora and Quinn."

"Loser."

"For wanting to spend time with my kid? And my—" What was Pandora? His girlfriend? Was he ready to take the next step and make her his fiancée? Guess in large part that depended on Julia. He couldn't even imagine how happy Pandora must be now that her daughter was back with her.

"Your what?"

"My girl—Pandora."

"I knew you were into her, but has it gone that far?" Though his friend's pinched expression clearly read he thought Calder was nuts, Calder didn't care. She meant the world to him. Being without her and his son all these months taught him he didn't want to leave again without knowing they'd both be waiting for him when he returned.

"If things go the way I think they will, pretty damn soon I might just make her my wife."

It was with that thought in mind, Calder approached his home—excited to see Quinn and Pandora, and of course, to finally meet Julia. He instinctively knew he and the little girl would become great friends. Hopefully, if he was lucky, she might even view him as her father one day.

It was 8:00 p.m. when Mason dropped him at the curb. Calder grabbed his gear, then mounted the front steps double-time to ring the bell.

He'd given Pandora his keys, just in case she decided it would be more practical for her and Quinn to *unofficially* live in Calder's home while he was deployed.

"Oh, my gosh! Harold!" Calder got a shock when his mom opened the door instead of Pandora. "Harold, come quick! Calder's home!"

"I'll be damned...." Harold rounded the corner from the living room to take Calder's ditty bag. "Welcome back. You've been sorely missed around here."

Inside, he found Quinn standing alongside the sofa, *eating* the remote. "Hey, bud, let's not do that, okay?" He swooped his son into his arms. "Man, you've grown." To his mom he said, "Bet he's walking real good now, huh?"

"Gah! Gah!"

"He walks a little too well. He still isn't formally talking, but he's into everything all the time. I'm exhausted."

"Phoooa!"

"Where's Pandora?" Calder checked the kitchen, then glanced down the hall.

"You haven't heard?"

"Heard what?" He was almost afraid to ask.

"Her court hearing went terribly. The judge put her off for another six months."

"That's ridiculous! Why?" Calder couldn't fathom the amount of pain she must be in.

"The judge didn't like the fact that she hadn't maintained a continuous address for the full six months he'd requested. Then Lila from down the street told me he got all bent out of shape about Pandora caring for your child when hers was taken away. What'd he call it in his written statement?" Finger to her mouth, she paused a moment to think. "Oh—duplicitous."

Sick didn't begin to describe the nausea building in Calder's stomach. Had he caused this? By overreacting to her past, forcing her to find a new place to live then making her look wishy-washy by so quickly leaving Quinn in her care upon realizing his mistake, had he ruined her court case?

"Her friend Natalie says poor Pandora has been inconsolable ever since. That's why she called us to watch Quinn."

"Sure," Calder said. "I understand." Doubling over, he braced his hands on his knees. "Wow, gotta say this is the last thing I expected."

"You should go to her. Don't worry about Quinn."

"Yeah. Thanks." He gave his son an extra-long hug, then hugged his mom and stepdad before heading to the garage for his bike.

PANDORA SAT ON her sofa alone in the dark.

No—wait. She wasn't entirely alone. As he had every night since she'd lost her hearing, her friend Jack sat on her lap—

Jack Daniel's, that is.

So far, the bottle was unopened, but in an odd way, holding it each night gave her strength. It proved that at least in one area of her life she still had control.

Had it really just been Thanksgiving when this very room had been filled with laughter and joy?

Her caseworker, Fran, had been as shocked by the hearing's outcome as she was and vowed to try breaking through red tape to expedite the legal process, but that was a pipe dream. Somewhere in all Pandora's newfound happiness, she'd forgotten the cardinal rule that had applied to most every day of her life up until finding her sobriety—she was a born loser. A societal outcast. She thought she could rise above her past, but at every turn, no matter how hard she tried, there it was, slithering right back to suck her down.

Car lights shone through the front window.

Having grown accustomed to the dark, she squinted at the intrusion.

When footfalls sounded on the steps, she cringed, praying whoever was there would go away.

The doorbell's peal offended her ears.

Then came banging. "Pandora! I know you're in there. Open the door!"

Calder?

"Go away!" It didn't matter how many nights she'd spent on this same sofa, praying for him to safely come home. Now that he was here, she'd say new prayers for him to leave.

"Open the damn door or I'll kick it in."

"I said, *go away!*"

He made good on his promise—only her flimsy lock hadn't needed much more than his powerful shoulder's nudge.

Rushing to her, he fixed his eyes on the bottle. "Oh, no, baby. Please, tell me you're not drinking again."

Clinging to the bottle, she looked up at him with tears in her eyes. "I—I want to."

He gently took the bottle from her, setting it on a side table. "I'm sorry I wasn't here for you, but I am now. I heard what happened with Julia. We'll fight this. There has to be a way."

"I—I *promised* her," she said with halting tears. "How many times can I let her down before she doesn't even want to be with me?"

"She has to know this isn't your fault."

"I w-wanted to talk to her, but the judge wouldn't let me. He said I was d-disorderly. B-but how would he feel if someone took his kid?"

Seated next to her, Calder lifted her onto his lap, holding her, cradling her, smoothing her hair. "We'll figure this out. That's a promise I'm making you. I wanted to wait for this, dream up some over-the-top surprise proposal—even ask Julia for her advice, but I say screw it. Let's get married right away. Tonight. Then, first thing in the morning, we'll get started on this as a united front." He kissed her tear-stained cheeks. "I know some pretty big names. They get things done. Trust me, baby. We'll get your daughter back."

She wanted to believe the fairy tale he was spinning, but trusting him was what first landed her in trouble.

"I—I want to believe you, but I c-can't." Pushing off him, she strode to the other side of the room, hugging herself, wishing he'd go away. "I want to blame you for all this. You firing me, making me move—I want to say that's what raised a red flag for the judge. But I'm a realist, Calder, and deep inside—" she patted her chest "—I know there's no one to blame for any of this but myself. I should never have even thought I could take on the responsibility of becoming a full-time nanny. How could I have been so stupid as to think the judge wouldn't have a problem with my holding that sort of position? And I should never have viewed working for you as anything more than a job. I shouldn't have fallen in love with Quinn."

"What about me?" Calder asked, striding her way, looking perilously handsome even in the shadows. "Did you fall in love with me, Pandora? Because I sure as hell feel that way about you."

"No, you don't," she said with a violent shake of her head. "You're in the business of saving people. You might think you love me, but all I am is one more mission for you to sweep in and fix. Nothing more. I wish I'd never even met you. Then I wouldn't have gotten the stupid idea in my head that the two of us ever stood a chance."

Calder had taken enough psychology courses in college to realize she didn't mean what she said and was only pushing him away out of fear he'd leave her, but that didn't make her hurtful words easier to bear.

He tried wrapping his arms around her, but she swatted him away. "Please, go. I don't need you. I don't need anyone. I'll buck up, get my head back in a good place then return to court in six more months and once and for all get my little girl."

"Okay. That's a great plan. But why not let me help?"

"Don't you see? I tried, Calder. I tried letting you in and it was a huge failure. Here you are, proposing marriage—in an incredibly lame, half-assed way—when what did we ever really share other than a few hot nights? You're a stranger. A stranger I made the mistake of falling for, and look where that's left me. For all I know, the only reason you even want me back is because you miss having a full-time sitter."

"That's B.S." Calder clenched his teeth so hard a muscle ticked in his jaw, and he found himself well and truly at a loss for words. Though he didn't just want her as an instant mom for Quinn, in other concerns, she was right. They did barely know each other. He'd never even learned the most basic facts—her favorite color or even her birthday.

What he had learned was that... *you know when you know.*

Calder had known Pandora was the woman for him all the way back from the day she'd literally saved his son's life. He'd known back when she'd first come to live with him and Quinn and she'd made him that delicious meat-loaf sandwich in the middle of the night. Pandora hadn't just saved Quinn but Calder, too. She'd taught him it was okay to commit. Because sometimes the people you love wind up loving you right back.

Only, where had all that newfound knowledge left him now?

"Calder, please," Pandora said, "I'm begging. Leave me alone. I got into this mess on my own, and I'll see my way out the same way. Whatever we shared, you know neither of us really meant it, so let's just end it now before our lives grow any more messy."

"You sure that's what you want?" Though she refused to make eye contact, she nodded.

He didn't have to be told twice.

Fighting his own tears, Calder granted Pandora's wish.

Chapter Seventeen

When Calder left, Pandora went to the window, watching him go. Had she just made the best or worst decision of her life? Maybe he could have helped bring Julia home. But if he couldn't? What if the judge perceived Calder's attempts to help as meddling? Pandora couldn't take the risk.

Without her jacket, Pandora grabbed her keys and purse.

She needed to get out of here. Speak to someone she trusted before making a grave mistake.

You don't trust Calder?

The real issue was not trusting herself around Calder.

It'd be so easy to lose herself to him. To abandon her every trouble, welcoming him to find solutions, but in the end, what would that say about her? She'd clawed her way from the edge of sanity to finally be in control. She couldn't come this far only to surrender to a man who may or may not stick around.

Her hands trembled so badly she had a hard time inserting her keys into the ignition.

Finally, she managed to get her car started, then she drove straight to Natalie.

"Get in here," her friend said when Pandora stood shivering at her front door.

To save money on utilities, Pandora had kept her heat low. Entering Natalie's home was what she'd always imagined the tropics must be. Balmy and serene—only with reggae playing instead of the latest TV ad from a Virginia Beach Chevy dealer blaring.

Natalie wrapped an afghan around Pandora's shoulders, ushering her to the sofa. "What's wrong?"

Tears began anew. "C-Calder's home. H-he asked me to marry him, but I can't. I have to stay strong to get Julia back. But to do that, I have to pull myself together." Covering her face with her hands, she admitted, "I can't eat or sleep. I'm so scared I'll never get Julia back."

"Calm down," Natalie urged. "I didn't want to say anything until we have a firm answer, but Anna and I, along with Lila and Martin and Gloria and Harold, have all chipped in to hire a *really* good lawyer who specializes in your type of case. We just need a smidge more money for his retainer, then—"

"No," Pandora said. "Please, don't give the judge any more cause to be upset. I need him to know I'm a good mom."

"You are," Natalie said. "You've learned your lesson. Everyone who loves you and has watched you grow into the woman you are today is ready for you to finally receive your ultimate reward—Julia."

"I will." Nodding, Pandora knew she would one day bring Julia home. She wouldn't have been able to survive without that core belief. "But look, I didn't come here to form some crazy takeover plan. I'm mortified by what happened in court. From here on out, I have to be perfect. I can't give that judge reason to believe I'm anything other than a textbook mom."

"That's all well and good," Natalie said, "but there's one problem."

"What's that?" Pandora sniffled.

"Outside of governmental guideline handbooks, I'm reasonably sure parental perfection doesn't exist. Parents make mistakes—granted, you made some doozies, but lucky for you, kids are resilient. Their most basic need is love. As long as you've got that covered, the rest will fall into place."

"Swell, but it doesn't change the fact that whether there's such a thing as a perfect parent or not, that's the standard I'm being held to."

CALDER SHOULD'VE GONE home after his blowout with Pandora, but knowing Quinn was no doubt in bed, as well as his parents, he wanted to kick back with his friends and a pitcher or two of beer. But then, how could he really even enjoy that, knowing alcohol sure as hell hadn't solved any of Pandora's problems?

Tipsea's was one of the last few places where a man could smoke in Norfolk, and Calder bought himself a cigar and two shots of whiskey at the bar. He'd seen the bottle at Pandora's and had fought a craving ever since. If he'd been with her, of course he'd have abstained, but since she'd booted him out on his ass, he figured why not get rip-roaring drunk?

What did he have to lose, anyway?

When it came to Pandora, everything was already lost.

"You're the last person I expected to see," Mason said.

Cooper trailed behind. "Why aren't you with Pandora and Quinn?"

"Kid's asleep and my woman dumped me." Calder signaled the barkeep for another shot.

"No way." Mason took the stool alongside him. "Thought you were about to propose."

"Me, too. But then I found out the court hearing for her to get her kid didn't go so great, and the night went downhill from there."

"Sure she's not just hurt and overreacting?" Cooper suggested.

Mason laughed. "Who appointed you the sensitivity police?"

"Shut up." Turning to Calder, Cooper said, "From the looks of you two at Thanksgiving, you were the real deal. Guess all I'm sayin' is I wouldn't just give up."

Calder clipped off the end of his cigar, then lit it. "Thank you, sir. I shall take that sage advice under advisement. Until then…" He raised his latest shot. "Let's toast to having the best damn night this side of Kandahar!"

IT WAS PUSHING 4:00 a.m. by the time Calder was sober enough to drive. He thought he was sneaking into the house, but as though he'd been caught in a time warp that had zapped him back to high school, his mom sat in the living room, awaiting his arrival.

"Big night out?" she asked, resting one of Pandora's old paperbacks on her lap.

"It was all right."

"Thought you were going to see Pandora."

"I did." He raked his fingers through his hair.

"And?"

Sighing, he said, "I don't mean to put you off, but it's been a seriously long day and I'm ready for bed." He headed for his room.

"Harold's in there. He snores so loud we've been sleeping separately. I set up camp in Pandora's old room."

"Where am I sleeping?"

His mom patted the couch.

He groaned. "Seriously?"

"We assumed you'd be staying with Pandora. We didn't just fall off the turnip truck, you know. We are acquainted with the birds and bees."

Blanching, he said, "Last thing I want to talk about with you is my sex life."

"Or lack thereof?" She laughed. "Why does everything seem so funny this late at night?"

He just shook his head.

"So really, what happened at Pandora's? She doesn't blame you for what happened in court, does she?"

"No." He sat hard on the sofa and scratched his head. "Mom, I opened up to her. I said we should get married, hire the best attorneys and tackle this thing together. But she's got a mile-long stubborn streak and insists on getting Julia back on her own."

"I meant to mention this to you earlier, but you ran out of here so fast I didn't have a chance. Pandora's friend Natalie has taken up a legal-fund collection. She planned on asking you to join as soon as you got back. What do you think?"

Sighing, he said what he most feared. "I think whatever demons Pandora's got inside won't let her accept what she deems charity. She takes full responsibility for the person she once was, and as such, seems to feel she's the only one who can bring Julia back into her life."

"The whole thing is awful. She's paid her dues and then some. Do you know she only spent six weeks in jail before being selected for the program that eventually helped turn her life around? I can't imagine how many parents drink themselves silly every night, yet they don't lose their children."

I was exactly that kind of parent tonight.

Calder asked, "What chance do you think we'd have of secretly helping her? Think the lawyer would talk to just us?"

"Seems to me we'll never know unless we ask."

"But, Mommy, why?" Julia asked on Pandora's first visit since losing her case. They cuddled together on the visitation room couch. Pandora had been reading, but Julia soon tired of that and instead wanted to talk. "You promised I could come home with you."

"I know, sweetie." Never had Pandora fought harder to maintain a bright smile. "But look at it this way, now you get to stay with Mom Cindy a little while longer. You like her, don't you?"

She hung her head. "Yeah, but not as much as you. She doesn't check around my bed for spiders."

"I'll bet if you asked, she would."

Julia said, "I guess. But I wanted to see my new room. And where's Quinn? Can't you bring him to visit?"

Where did Pandora begin to explain what had happened between her and Quinn's dad? How she'd give anything if whatever she and Calder shared could've worked? But it hadn't. And if she were honest with herself, Pandora had known from the start it wouldn't.

Men like Calder didn't fall for disasters like her.

"Mommy?"

"Yes?"

"Why does that judge hate us?" The knot in Pandora's throat threatened to seal off her vocal cords.

"Sweetie, he doesn't hate us—especially not you." She swept hair from in front of her daughter's eyes, tucking it behind her ears. "Remember how I told you I made bad mistakes?"

"Uh-huh…."

"Well, like when you do something naughty at school and need a time-out—"

Julia looked up. "I'm never bad at school."

"Okay, well, you know how some kids are bad at school? And they get in trouble, but then everything's okay? Well, the judge says I'm still in trouble."

"But it's been a long time. I'm tired of you being in detention." Her daughter snuggled closer. "Please, take me home with you. I don't like coming here."

In her peripheral vision, Pandora caught the woman supervising their visit jotting something in her notebook.

Her stomach sank.

WEEKS PASSED.

Each day when Calder brought Quinn to the day care and then returned to pick up his son, Pandora scurried to avoid him. She dashed for the bathroom or ducked into the supply closet. The few times he'd caught her off guard, she'd found herself instantly overcome by sadness and grief and the kind of longing that stemmed from knowing she'd once almost had something special but had lost it.

Luckily, today she'd made it to the janitor's closet in the nick of time.

She stood in the dark, slowly counting to five hundred, which she figured should be a reasonable enough time for Calder to be on his way.

Finished, she opened the door to find him there, facing her with his hands tucked in his pockets.

"How long are you planning on playing this game, Pandora?"

"I—I don't know what you mean." She fussed with her hair, certain after playing with the kids all day she must be a mess.

"Can you honestly tell me you're better off without me? That you don't think about how great the two of us could've been?"

"Calder, please…." She looked at her chipped nail polish.

"Please, what? Hold you? Kiss you?" He'd stepped close enough for his warm breath to fan her cheeks. He smelled of the chocolate-chip cookies Pandora had baked for the front entry's reception counter.

She notched her chin higher. "I meant, please go." *Before I lose my last shred of resistance where you're concerned.* Did he have any idea how many nights she'd lain awake, staring at her ceiling, struggling with her decision to let him go? Of course, she'd done the right thing. Her sole focus in life must be centered on getting her daughter back. But every once in a while, on particularly cold, blustery nights, her thoughts drifted to him. That one magical night he'd held her, and how for those precious few hours everything had seemed okay.

"Today," he said with a funny smile she couldn't recall ever having seen, "I'll do as you ask, but one of these days, Pandora, you're going to be begging me to stay."

Unable to meet his intense gaze, she looked at her feet, mumbling, "Please, Calder, no more teasing. You really need to go."

CONTACTING A HIGH-PRICED attorney had only gotten Calder so far. To achieve the results he truly needed, he'd have to call in the big guns, which is why he now sat somewhere he never thought he would—in one of the base commander's two burgundy leather guest chairs.

"As a matter of fact, I do know someone who may be able to help." The white-haired man spun his enormous old-school Rolodex, stopping it on the *T*s. "Let me see…." He fingered through card after card. "Ah—here he is. Old buddy of mine from Annapolis. Thought he might be SEAL material, but he broke his leg skiing in Vermont and that was that. Glorious career down the tubes before it even started. Anyway, give him a call, explain your situation. He's the type who gets things done."

Calder took the proffered card. "Thank you, sir. Keep me in mind if you ever need a favor."

The commander laughed. "Don't let my wife hear that."

THE FIRST WEEK in May, Pandora grabbed the mail, then climbed the stairs to her apartment, tilting her face to the last of the day's warm sun.

It'd been a rough day at work. There'd been a fight in the three-year-old room over a toy truck and she'd noticed a speech therapist had come to see Quinn, who still hadn't said a formal word beyond *uh-oh*.

She'd had Natalie speak to Calder about working with him at night. Dinner or bath times were great for word reinforcement—pointing at specific items and repeating the name at least three times.

Inside, she set the mail on the counter and made a quick trip to the restroom, then her bedroom to change.

Back in the kitchen, she filled the kettle with water and set it on the stove to boil. While waiting for her steaming mug of chamomile tea to cool, she finally got around to flipping through the mail.

An envelope with the return address of Judge B. Thomas Thornton in the top left corner sent her pulse racing. She tore into it, fearing a further setback to her case, only to instead release a squeak.

How had this happened? What had happened?

The judge wanted to see her in his chambers to discuss his ruling—in two days!

She called Natalie to ask if she'd ever heard of anything like this before. She hadn't.

Her next call was to Lila, who also reported that the letter sounded odd, but that Pandora should cross her fingers for something positive to happen.

The next two days, Pandora wasn't sure what to do with the emotions balling in her stomach. On the one hand, maybe the judge had decided he'd been too hard on her and figured she should regain custody of her daughter. The more realistic view was that he'd discovered a bureaucratic loophole that would assign permanent custody of Julia to her foster family.

The mere thought made her nauseous.

More than anything, she wanted to phone Calder. Hear his take on what the judge could possibly want.

No matter how sad she might sometimes be over losing him, she had only to envision her daughter to realize no sacrifice was too big when it came to bringing Julia home. Calder had become a distraction when every ounce of her energy needed to be focused on her beautiful little girl.

For Pandora's newest court date, she'd asked Natalie for the afternoon off. That morning had been never ending, and when the time came to leave, her friend was nowhere to be found.

Odd. Since Natalie had been with her for most of her legal journey, why now, when anything could happen, would she be MIA?

She tried Lila, thinking she'd like to have at least one of her friends there for her in case she received even worse news than she had her last day in court, but not even Martin answered their house phone.

Alone and frightened, Pandora proceeded to court.

Should something truly awful happen, she'd deal with it then. For now, she had to stay strong. She could not suffer the kind of emotional breakdown she had the last time she'd been here.

The judge's chambers were located on a different floor from the courtroom. Pandora found it odd her meeting would be there.

She announced herself to a secretary who pointed her to a row of wooden chairs. "The judge will be with you momentarily."

Dozens of thoughts raced through Pandora's head. What if she lost permanent custody of Julia? What if she'd broken some arcane law she wasn't even aware of and was being carted off to prison? What if—

"Ms. Moore, the judge will see you now."

With her pulse racing, her breathing erratic and her palms sweating, Pandora smoothed her dress, then followed the middle-aged woman into a heavily paneled room.

"Ah, the famous Ms. Moore." The judge rose, gesturing for her to have a seat. "I've been on the bench twenty years and never have I heard such a ruckus."

"I don't know what you mean." She sat primly with her hands neatly folded on her lap, praying her galloping pulse could only be heard by her.

"You're not spearheading this campaign?" He tapped a file she presumed was hers.

"No, sir. I honestly don't know why I'm here."

"Humph." He shook his head. "Might as well get on with it. Ms. Moore, whether you're aware of it or not, you have quite a few friends in high places. They've convinced me to take a second look at your case and I'm ashamed to admit, upon closer inspection, you truly are the kind of woman many in the system should aspire to be."

"Th-thank you." The judge's praise made Pandora's chest squeeze with apprehension. He wouldn't be building her up only to tear her down again, would he?

"In light of this, and my earlier mistake, please accept my heartfelt apology and know your pain has at least filled one purpose—I'll now be taking a more common-sense approach to all my hearings. You really are a wonder. Ms. Pandora Moore, I hereby grant you full and permanent custody of one minor child, Miss Julia Elizabeth Moore." He lightly slammed his desk with his gavel. "Case dismissed." Rising, he pointed toward a door. "You might want to greet the lot hiding out in there."

Dazed, unsure if she could be dreaming, Pandora asked, "Really? I'm done? Julia's mine?"

"She's really and truly yours." After patting her back, he

opened the door to a secondary waiting area for her. "Job well done, Ms. Moore."

"Mommy!" Julia was first into her arms, then Natalie and Anna, Lila and Martin, even her caseworker, Fran. Everyone was laughing and talking and Pandora couldn't stop happy tears.

"Sweetie," Pandora said while hugging her daughter, "I love you so much."

"I love you, too."

Once the initial excitement wore down and they all left the judge's chambers, Pandora caught sight of two familiar, dear faces. Calder and Quinn.

They'd reached the lobby where Julia said her goodbyes to teary Mom Cindy.

Pandora said to Calder, "You did this, didn't you?"

He shrugged. "I helped, but so did everyone else. We *all* love you. When you told me the judge denied you custody, I refused to believe for one second we couldn't turn this around."

"We?" She was almost afraid to ask.

"Woman, if you're going to be in a relationship with a SEAL, there's one thing you need to learn up front."

"What's that?" As much as she'd tried telling herself she no longer wanted him, she did. Being near him brought on a fierce longing she was no longer capable of denying.

"We *never* quit. We're like human bulldozers—mowing down anything—anyone—in our way to make the seemingly impossible happen."

"Mommy?" Julia asked, hopping up and down. "May I please hold Quinn?"

"You know my son?" Calder asked Julia.

Her daughter nodded. "Mommy brought him to see me. He's cute. I love babies. My foster mom, Cindy, just had a baby girl and I helped her a lot."

"That's nice of you." He extended his hand. "I'm Calder. I've heard an awful lot of nice things about you."

She giggled. "Mommy says you're nice, too."

"Really?" He raised his eyebrows, glancing Pandora's way.

"Yep!" Julia gave an exaggerated nod.

Pandora gathered their group together as she stood with Julia's backside against her, hugging her arms around her daughter's chest. "I'm not sure what part each of you played in making this miracle happen, but I don't know how to begin to thank you." She was crying again, but happy tears sure beat the heck out of her usual despondency. "For as long as I live, I'll never forget what you've done."

Her speech was ended by more tears and hugs and smiles.

An impromptu party popped up at Pandora's apartment, making her glad she'd long since finished Julia's room.

While Natalie and Anna ran out for burger fixings and Lila and Martin went briefly home to let out a vacationing neighbor's dog, Pandora showed Julia her new room. "Do you like it?"

"It's so pretty! I love the stuffed animals!"

"We still have to find a place for the nice things your foster family bought, but I'm sure we'll manage."

Julia explored the rest of the apartment, ending in the kitchen, where she spotted her coloring page on the fridge. "Hey! I made that!"

"You sure did, angel. Think you can make more?"

"Yeah! Want me to start now?"

Pandora laughed. "If you'd like. But don't forget it's a school night. Do you have any homework from missing today?"

She sighed. "A little. Do I have to do it now?"

Pandora hated jumping right into the least fun part of parenting, but she'd worked a long time to be in this position and she wasn't about to ruin it now. "Yes, I really think it'd be best to get it out of the way. Come on—" she patted the table "—I'll help. Then you'll have it over with and can enjoy your party."

"Okay." While Julia ran to her room to gather books and supplies, Pandora fixed a small snack tray of apple slices and peanut butter.

Being a mom again made Pandora feel as close to being whole as she had in a while. The only thing missing she wasn't even sure could be replaced. One thing was for certain. Now that her primary dream had come true, it was time to start on another....

That is, assuming Calder and Quinn were amenable.

CALDER MOUNTED THE stairs to Pandora's apartment, not quite sure why he was even there. The last time he'd visited her in her home she'd pushed him away. He'd understood her reasoning, but that hadn't lessened the hurt embedded by her words. The doubt that'd always been with him now dogged him even more.

"Remember what we practiced?" he asked his son, who'd insisted on climbing the stairs on his own. "Pan-door-rah?"

"Eee-boo!" Quinn called.

Calder held his hand, reminding Quinn on each new step of the word he was supposed to say. Each night there were also many other words—boat, soap, peas, pig, dog—the list went on and on.

The screen door shot open and Julia popped out. "Mommy! Quinn's here and his dad!" She bolted down the stairs. "Hi!"

"Hey. I sure am glad to see you here. Having fun with your mom?"

Quinn grunted his way up the last few steps.

"Uh-huh. But I had to do my math for tomorrow. But she helped, so it wasn't too bad."

"I used to hate homework. But then I figured out the faster I got it done, the faster I got to play."

She laughed. "I never thought of it like that! Can I play with Quinn?"

"Sure. But let's get him inside first."

"Okay!"

Calder found Pandora at the sink, peeling potatoes.

"Hey." To keep from pulling her into a hug, he rammed his hands into his pockets.

"May I play with Quinn now?" Julia asked.

"You certainly may," Calder answered. "Be careful with him, though."

"I will. Come on—" she took Quinn by the hand "—come see my room. It's really cool."

Alone with Pandora, Calder felt tongue-tied.

"I'm making potato salad," she said. "Would you mind grabbing a couple pots—one big and one little—and filling them with water to boil?"

"Have you always been this bossy?" he couldn't resist teasing. It'd be so easy falling into their old comfortable routine. He'd missed that closeness. The sense of having someone who knew him inside and out—only, that was the funny thing about him and Pandora. On the surface, they hardly knew each other, but deep down he felt as if he'd known her a lifetime.

"Probably not." She shyly ducked her gaze, in the process spilling her hair forward, baring the spot on her neck he used to love to nuzzle.

There was an awkward shuffle as he did her bidding, trying not to touch her but wanting to so badly.

"Calder?" She lifted her glasses, resting them atop her head.

"Yes?"

She blew out a deep breath. "I'm sorry. I said horrible

things to you, but I was so afraid." She bowed her head again, but then looked up, dazzling him with her sweet, unaffected smile. "I told you I didn't blame you—*us*—for my court hearing going wrong, but deep inside, part of me did. That was wrong. Bottom line—I wasn't thinking. All I can say is being without Julia made me temporarily insane."

"And now?"

There she went again with that smile. "I once asked you for a second chance…" She flopped her hands at her sides. "Here I am again. Y-you asked me to marry you, and I'm not ready for that—it wouldn't be fair to my daughter—but breathing one more second without you and Quinn in my life isn't fair to me. Today at the courthouse, when I saw you and realized what you'd done, it hit me how stupid it was of me to ever think I wanted to live the rest of my life alone. Why, you know? When it's so much better with friends."

Calder pulled her into the hug he'd craved since that morning, and then he slid his hands into her hair, kissing her with an urgency he didn't bother trying to hide.

"I love you," she said. "I think I've loved you from the day you rescued me at the grocery store."

He kissed her again. "I've loved you since you saved my baby from choking on that grape."

"Quinn choked on a grape?" Julia wandered in with Quinn in tow. "Is he okay?"

Sniffling from still more happy tears, Pandora said, "He's amazing."

"When we were in my room," Julia said, "Quinn was trying to talk. Has he said any words yet?"

"Nope." Calder slipped his arm around Pandora's waist. "What did he say?"

"It sounded like pan. Does he like playing with pots and pans?" She ran to a cupboard and pulled out a pan and its lid. Clanging it, she asked Quinn, "Pan? Were you trying to say pan?"

Calder crossed his fingers. *Kid, if you ever wanted to wow a crowd, now would be the time.*

"Well, mister?" Pandora knelt in front of him, taking his hands. "Do you finally have something to say?"

"Pan! Pand!"

"He did say it!" Julia gave her pans another clang. "Do it again!"

"Pando!"

Puzzled, Pandora asked, "Is he trying to say panda? Calder, he doesn't have a stuffed panda, does he?"

"Not that I can think of."

"Pandor! Pando!"

Julia clapped. "He's so cute!"

"Calder?" Pandora asked. "Can you make out what he's saying?"

He shrugged. *Come on, little guy. Say it. Say it.* "Beats me. Wouldn't have a clue."

Quinn ran from Julia to Pandora, then he held up his hands, pinching his fingers. *"Pan-door-ah! Pan-door-ah!"*

She covered her mouth with her hands and tears shone in her eyes. "No way. How would he ever have learned my name?" She looked to Calder, who couldn't hide his smile. "Have you been coaching him all this time?"

"Pan-door-rah!"

She lifted him, spinning around and hugging him. "You're such a brilliant boy!"

"Takes after his father," Calder noted.

"Yes, he does." Pandora, with Quinn still in her arms, leaned close to Calder to kiss his cheek. "You've already given me one amazing gift today. Now two? How am I ever going to repay you?"

"That's the thing about gifts—" he pulled Pandora, Julia

and Quinn into his arms "—there's no need to ever repay them. But if you'd want to be my girl, I am accepting applications."

"In that case…" She winked. "I'd better grab a pen."

Epilogue

"Three, two, one! Happy New Year!" Pandora danced and cheered and hugged with Julia and Quinn, but she saved her kiss for her husband.

"I love you, Mr. Remington."

"I love you, Mrs. Remington." Because of her bulging baby bump, Pandora struggled to reach her arms all the way around Calder. At the end of her six-month lease, they'd moved back into Calder's home, but because of their still-growing family, they were in the process of selling that house and looking for something larger.

All their friends had squeezed inside for the night. Natalie and Anna, Lila and Martin, Gloria and Harold, Patricia and Heath, Cooper and Mason, along with many of the other men on Calder's SEAL team, as well as their wives.

The biggest surprise of all was realizing what a small world it was when encountering her former counselor Ellie, who'd married Calder's friend, Deacon. She and Ellie hugged it out, with Pandora apologizing for having given her such a hard time. Ellie warmed Pandora's heart by thanking her for proving her volunteer work really did make an eventual difference by touching lives.

"Where are you?" Calder asked as they danced to "Auld Lang Syne."

"Just thinking what an amazing life we've built in such a short time. I feel reborn." She kissed him. "All thanks to you."

"You've done a lot for me, too, you know." With his hands low on her hips, she wouldn't be too sad when the party was over. If the kids cooperated, they'd finally be alone.

"Oh, yeah?" she teased. "Like what?"

"Let's see." He stopped dancing to touch his finger to his lips as if feigning deep thought. "I'll always be grateful for your meat loaf...."

That earned him a swat. "I'm trying to be serious."

"Oh, Mrs. Remington, I'm very serious. And to prove it, look what I found under your snowflake ice sculpture—it chipped off." He slipped a sparkling square-cut gold-and-diamond solitaire onto her left-hand ring finger, nestling it alongside her gold wedding band.

"Calder?" She released him to put her hands over her mouth. "You're crazy! I don't need this. We talked about how all our savings needed to go into the new house."

"Unless you're planning on leaving your hand behind, by that definition, the ring will move right along with us."

Pandora hated how her pregnancy had her crying more than ever, but she'd say this was just cause. When they'd married, the legal fees incurred from bringing Julia back into her life had prevented Calder from affording an engagement ring.

"Besides, Heath took me to the same guy he bought Patricia's ring from and he gave me an awesome military discount."

"I still say you're crazy."

He grabbed her left hand and tugged at her new sparkler. "Want me to take it back?"

"No." She kissed her ring, then him. "I love this ring,

but most of all, I love you. Thank you, Calder, for saving my life."

He winked before flashing his slow, sexy grin. "I'm a SEAL. That's what I do."

* * * * *

Be sure to look for the next book in
Laura Marie Altom's OPERATION: FAMILY series,
THE SEAL'S CHRISTMAS TWINS,
available in December 2013!

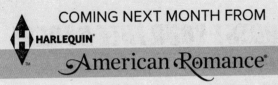

REQUEST YOUR FREE BOOKS!
2 FREE NOVELS PLUS 2 FREE GIFTS!

HARLEQUIN®

American ★ Romance®

LOVE, HOME & HAPPINESS

YES! Please send me 2 FREE Harlequin® American Romance® novels and my 2 FREE gifts (gifts are worth about $10). After receiving them, if I don't wish to receive any more books, I can return the shipping statement marked "cancel." If I don't cancel, I will receive 4 brand-new novels every month and be billed just $4.74 per book in the U.S. or $5.24 per book in Canada. That's a savings of at least 14% off the cover price! It's quite a bargain! Shipping and handling is just 50¢ per book in the U.S. and 75¢ per book in Canada.* I understand that accepting the 2 free books and gifts places me under no obligation to buy anything. I can always return a shipment and cancel at any time. Even if I never buy another book, the two free books and gifts are mine to keep forever.

154/354 HDN F4YN

Name _____ (PLEASE PRINT) _____

Address _____ Apt. # _____

City _____ State/Prov. _____ Zip/Postal Code _____

Signature (if under 18, a parent or guardian must sign)

Mail to the **Harlequin® Reader Service:**
IN U.S.A.: P.O. Box 1867, Buffalo, NY 14240-1867
IN CANADA: P.O. Box 609, Fort Erie, Ontario L2A 5X3

Want to try two free books from another line?
Call 1-800-873-8635 or visit www.ReaderService.com.

* Terms and prices subject to change without notice. Prices do not include applicable taxes. Sales tax applicable in N.Y. Canadian residents will be charged applicable taxes. Offer not valid in Quebec. This offer is limited to one order per household. Not valid for current subscribers to Harlequin American Romance books. All orders subject to credit approval. Credit or debit balances in a customer's account(s) may be offset by any other outstanding balance owed by or to the customer. Please allow 4 to 6 weeks for delivery. Offer available while quantities last.

Your Privacy—The Harlequin® Reader Service is committed to protecting your privacy. Our Privacy Policy is available online at www.ReaderService.com or upon request from the Harlequin Reader Service.

We make a portion of our mailing list available to reputable third parties that offer products we believe may interest you. If you prefer that we not exchange your name with third parties, or if you wish to clarify or modify your communication preferences, please visit us at www.ReaderService.com/consumerschoice or write to us at Harlequin Reader Service Preference Service, P.O. Box 9062, Buffalo, NY 14269. Include your complete name and address.

HAR13R

A sixth sense told Conway he was being watched. He opened his eyes beneath the cowboy hat covering his face. Two pairs of small athletic shoes stood side by side next to the sofa.

"Is he dead?"

"Poke him and see," whispered a second voice.

Conway shifted on the couch and groaned.

"He's alive."

"Maybe he's sick."

"Look under his hat."

"You look."

Conway's chest shook with laughter. Small fingers lifted the brim of his hat and suddenly Conway's gaze clashed with the boys'. They shrieked and jumped back.

He pointed to one kid. "What's your name?"

"Javier."

Conway moved his finger to the other boy.

"I'm Miguel. Who are you?"

"Conway Cash."

Javier whispered in his brother's ear, then Miguel asked, "Why are you sleeping on our couch?"

"Your mom wasn't feeling well, so I stayed the night."

"Javi…Mig…. Where are you guys?" Isi's sluggish voice rang out a moment before she appeared in the hallway.

"Mom, Conway Cash slept on our couch."

"It was nice of Mr. Conway to stay, but I'm fine now." Isi sent him a time-to-leave look.

Conway stood and handed her a piece of paper. "Your sitter left this for you last night. She wanted you to read it first thing in the morning."

While Isi read the note, Conway said, "I'd really like to make it up to you for what happened last night. Is there anything I can—"

Isi glanced up from the note, a stunned expression on her face.

"What's wrong?" he asked.

"Nicole quit. She's moving to Tucson to live with her father."

"Maybe your mother could help out with the boys."

"I told you a long time ago that I don't have any family. It's just me and the boys." She paused. "You offered to help. Would you watch the boys until I find a replacement sitter?"

Babysit? Him? "I don't think that's a good idea."

"It would be for two or three days at the most."

"I don't know anything about kids."

"Never mind." Her shoulders sagged.

Oh, hell. How hard could it be to watch a couple of four-year-olds? "Okay, I'll watch them."

She flashed him a bright smile. "You'll need to be here by noon on Monday."

"See you then." Right now, Conway couldn't escape fast enough.

Find out if Conway survives his new babysitting duties in
TWINS UNDER THE CHRISTMAS TREE
by Marin Thomas
Available October 1, 2013, only from
Harlequin® American Romance®.

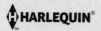
HARLEQUIN®

American Romance®

A rancher comes to her rescue.

At the magnificent Wyoming dude ranch run by
Ross Livingston and two fellow ex-marines, families
of fallen soldiers find hope and healing. When lovely
widow Kit Wentworth and her son arrive, Ross
immediately finds himself drawn to them. Soon he's
able to bring young Andy out of his shell—and touch
Kit's heart as no other man has.

Her Wyoming Hero
by REBECCA WINTERS

Available October 1, 2013, only from
Harlequin® American Romance®.

HAR75475